LOST ENCHANTMENT

Eden resolved that Dane, her estranged husband, should know all about their six-year-old son Jonathan—the son he had never even met. But how would that affect Dane's estrangement from her?

Books you will enjoy
by MARGARET PARGETER

TOTAL SURRENDER

Neale Curtis had taken an instant dislike to her boss, Lawton Baillie. Until she was forced to join him on his yacht, when her feelings began to change—but that was dangerous, because he had made it perfectly clear what *he* wanted, and it wasn't what she wanted . . .

CAPTIVE OF FATE

Brice claimed he would never trust Macy again. What chance, then, did their marriage have?

MODEL OF DECEPTION

Paula's objective in going to the Caribbean was to persuade Luke Armstrong to sell his island there. And everything seemed to be going according to plan until Luke turned the tables on her in way she hadn't bargained for!

IMPASSE

Five years after they had parted, Lee Moreau and Slade Western had met again—and Lee soon realised that all her old love for Slade had come back too. But now she was engaged to nice, kind Matt Leland. How could she hurt him by leaving him for a man who wasn't even offering her marriage?

LOST ENCHANTMENT

BY

MARGARET PARGETER

MILLS & BOON LIMITED
15–16 BROOK'S MEWS
LONDON W1A 1DR

First published in Great Britain 1985
by Mills & Boon Limited

© Margaret Pargeter 1985

Australian copyright 1985
Philippine copyright 1985
This edition 1985

ISBN 0 263 75119 8

Set in Monophoto Times 10 on 10½ pt.
01–0885 - 60209

Made and printed in Great Britain by
Richard Clay (The Chaucer Press) Ltd,
Bungay, Suffolk

CHAPTER ONE

EDEN looked at her five-year-old son and asked if he was sure he wanted to go to France with his grandparents?

'I think so,' he answered, with a kind of doubtful eagerness on his small face. 'It's nice there but I wish you were coming too.'

Eden closed her eyes briefly, reluctant to be reminded each year of another summer when she and Dane had been two of the Britons hurtling in pursuit of the sun along the autoroutes to the Mediterranean.

Feeling shaken but aware of Jonathan's gaze on her, she blinked and said firmly. 'It will only be for two weeks and you know I can't leave the shop.'

'Gran says there's nothing to stop you,' he retorted, his still babyish mouth pouting.

'Jonathan!' Eden's expression told him more clearly than words that she didn't approve of such talk. 'Gran doesn't understand but you should. I have to work to keep us and I can't do that if I take time off whenever I feel like it. Gran shouldn't make such remarks in front of you but you should know better than to listen.'

He frowned. 'Gran says, since you aren't married now . . .'

'That's enough, Jonathan!' Eden exclaimed, refusing to listen to a boy of five-and-a-half repeating things he probably didn't entirely understand but which he should never have heard in the first place. It wasn't likely that her mother had been discussing her divorce with him but that she had obviously been discussing it with someone within earshot, made Eden mad. Why couldn't her mother accept that, after Dane, she was in no hurry to commit herself again. She was tired of her mother pointing out that Eden wasn't getting any younger and that Trevor Lawson might not be content to wait forever. Trevor didn't have to wait for her—she had never asked him to, or to pursue her as he did. She was ready to admit there were occasions when she appreciated his company but she was nowhere near ready to marry him—yet.

When Jonathan, looking sulkier than ever, asked if he might watch television, she gave her permission. With the lounge door safely closed behind him, she rang home and spoke to her mother. 'You can have him for two weeks,' she consented, 'but no longer.'

That Irene Spencer resented the time limit imposed by her daughter was revealed by her cool tones as she asked, 'How do you intend managing for the rest of the holidays? Really, Eden . . .'

'Mrs Willis still comes in,' Eden interrupted curtly, 'and when she isn't able to, he can come to the shop with me.'

'But it's all so unnecessary!' Irene wailed. 'If only you would be sensible and marry Trevor, you could forget about the shop. It's years since your divorce and Jonathan needs a father.'

'Mother, please, not again!' Eden did her best to keep her temper. She would be worn to a frazzle if she lost it every time her mother got on to her favourite subject and she hadn't yet found a permanent way of shutting her up.

'If you hadn't married that man . . .'

Eden banged down the 'phone with no consideration for her mother's ears. Irene never gave up. Being utterly ruthless was the only way of achieving some respite, if only temporarily. Escaping from her after Jonathan's birth and living on her own had made little difference. She persisted, like a dripping tap, until frequently Eden felt like screaming. 'Marry Trevor,' she'd advise. 'He's rich and could keep you in comfort, as your father did, before you married that penniless Dane Sutherland.'

Dane wasn't penniless. From odd bits of information, gleaned from newspapers, he wasn't now, anyway, but there was no denying he had been when she had married him. She had been eighteen, Dane over ten years older and struggling to establish himself in the oil business, with no real time to spare for the marriage neither he nor her parents had wanted.

Bitterly Eden reflected, as she began preparing the simple supper she usually gave Jonathan at six o'clock, that a lot of good getting her own way had done her in the long run! She hadn't been nineteen when she was divorced and just six months over it when Jonathan had been born, the son of a man who almost certainly didn't know of his existence. Her marriage had brought her nothing but pain and disillusionment and she definitely wasn't going to allow her mother to push her into another which she feared might end just as disastrously.

The next morning, being Sunday, her mother rang. Despite their near quarrel of yesterday, Eden wasn't surprised. Irene prided herself on never bearing a grudge though both Eden and her father knew this was only when it suited her. Eden hadn't lived for twenty-five years without learning to recognise her mother's deviousness but it never really bothered her. She was only afraid that Irene, with plenty of time on her hands, might one day, conceivably, succeed in out-smarting her over Jonathan.

'We'll expect you for lunch as usual, darling,' Irene purred. 'Your father is sending Briggs for you and don't forget Jonathan's things, will you? He must stay with us, overnight, as we shall be leaving early in the morning.'

Which might easily mean afternoon and her mother could have picked Jonathan up from here. Eden gave in with bad grace. 'I'd just as soon have given lunch a miss, today, but if you insist . . .'

'I do,' Irene murmured, sounding even more like a cat with some cream.

Eden realised why when she saw Trevor was one of the guests.

'You'll be able to see more of each other without

Jonathan underfoot,' Irene smiled innocently while
Jonathan was out in the grounds, playing.

Trevor nodded, a cunning gleam in his eyes. 'Perhaps
I'll be able to pursuade her to come with me and join
you for a long weekend, Irene?'

'No thank you,' Eden was determined to squash any
such notion in the bud, 'St Tropez is not for me at this
time of year.'

'I adore it!' Irene sighed rapturously.

'Because it's full of designer labels and frivolous
fashions and friends,' her daughter retorted tartly.

'Isn't Eden unkind!' Irene appealed to Trevor
plaintively.

'She's too beautiful to be really unkind,' Trevor said,
with a lack of logic that set Eden's teeth on edge. 'But I
know what you mean.'

Certain of an ally, Irene continued resentfully. 'It's
not as if the villa was in the middle of town.'

'Beautifully secluded,' Trevor agreed.

'It's really ridiculous,' Eden retorted, 'to own a house
you only use for a few weeks each year.'

'We loan it to friends.'

Eden sighed and went to talk to her father. He was
better, if not much. Like her mother, he thought money
could buy anything and held firmly to the belief that
those who earned it had the right to spend it as they
wished. He had never forgiven Dane for refusing to let
it buy him. Still, the years had mellowed him, he had
grown more tolerant, and Eden had an idea that he had
altered his opinion of Dane.

Damn the man! Because, for some reason, Dane
wouldn't stay out of her thoughts this weekend, she
tossed back the thick braid of fair hair, that wouldn't
stop slipping over her shoulders, with unjustifiable
impatience and began talking to Richard Spencer about
his garden.

Later, Trevor took her out to dinner and ended the
evening with another proposal. 'I'm sorry, Trevor,' she
replied, wondering how many times he had asked,

which might have told her how many times she'd refused him.

'You can't go on saying no forever.' Trevor's fair brows drew together as he locked his expensive car before following Eden into the flat. The road outside smelled of melting tar, the buildings of decay and peeling paint. The way he slammed the door indicated what he thought of the neighbourhood where Eden lived. He looked no better pleased when Eden replied that she could and that he mustn't stay long. She was tired.

'It's that confounded shop,' he snapped, accepting her excuse rather than believe she wished to be rid of him. 'It's not as if it was an ordinary shop either,' he grumbled. 'Antiques, I ask you! If you sold ordinary merchandise it would be delivered from the factory to your door, but, as it is, you have to go out and look for the stuff you sell then buy it and sell it all over again. Or pay someone to do it for you.'

If Eden hadn't felt so annoyed, she might have been amused by the way he described how she worked. 'I might remind you,' she said tersely, 'that what I choose to do is my own business and one can't exist without money.'

He sighed long and patiently. 'All I'm trying to point out is that I make enough money to keep both you and Jonathan in luxury.'

'You mean your father does.'

'Your parents are rolling in it too,' he returned with retaliatory frankness. 'We could be set up for life if only you'd marry me.'

Why couldn't she? Eden gazed at him blindly but didn't miss his extremely presentable appearance. He was a few years older than herself and had adored her even before she met Dane. 'Perhaps one day . . .' she murmured, for the first time wondering if she could bring herself to give in? He liked Jonathan and if Jonathan wasn't too struck on him, he was used to him. However, she wasn't deciding anything tonight!

'You have to give me time,' she shrugged, without realising how ludicrous that sounded after so many years.

Trevor, though, was so impressed at having gained even this small concession that he wasn't inclined to argue. Exercising what he considered commendable restraint, he nodded agreeably and began talking of other things. At ten, after a last drink, he departed readily enough when he was asked to. He really wasn't bad, Eden thought affectionately as she closed the door and promptly forgot him.

The flat seemed empty after he had gone and without Jonathan. Moodily, Eden wandered around it, disinclined to go straight to bed and unable to shake off a feeling of depression. Sometimes she felt lonely, living on her own. After Jonathan had arrived, in a frantic search for independence, she hadn't deluded herself into thinking it would be easy. She knew she had been fortunate in finding four small but adequate rooms, with a woman downstairs willing to look after a baby. She had also been fortunate in finding a job with the owner of an antique shop. She must have seemed an unlikely candidate for such a position, a divorced girl of nineteen with a small baby, but Eden had haunted antique shops for years and Lydia Granger had learned to recognise natural talent when she saw it. Then, three years ago, when Lydia had moved on, Eden had managed to take over the business with the help of a small legacy from her grandfather. Business had boomed. It might not be an ideal way of earning a living but it did provide financial independence and the hard work involved prevented her from dwelling too much on other things. It was only when she was alone in the flat, as she was now, that these other things returned to torment her. With an impatient sigh, she marched into the small kitchen to make herself a cup of cocoa, hoping it would help her to sleep.

The following evening, the shop was closed and she was listening with half an ear to the six o'clock news as she checked various things, when the newscaster paused and suddenly announced.

'Word has just come in from one of the major oil companies in the Shetlands, of an accident on one of their North Sea rigs. Two men have been killed and Dane Sutherland, the man directing operations, is believed to be seriously injured. We hope to bring you more on this later.'

The voice went on, leaving Eden in a state of shock. Dane seriously injured. Oh God, no! Her face went grey as she sank helplessly down on a Regency chair and buried her face in her hands. Dane and she might be divorced but divorce didn't necessarily kill all feelings. And Jonathan was his son.

'Oh, no!' she moaned again, this time aloud. He didn't know he had a son, for she had never told him. She had tried to, when she had gone into hospital, a week before Jonathan was born. She had written a letter and given it to Trevor to post. Her mother had been so against her marriage that she couldn't have trusted her to post it. After waiting for a reply in vain, she had written again, a few days after Jonathan arrived. In both letters she had merely said she was ill and had some news for him, but he had neither come himself, nor had she heard from him. And he must have received her letters for she had sent them to his company to be forwarded to him. She recalled how, despite everything, she had longed for him, a longing that had grown numb during the following years until it had gradually disappeared.

In panic she jumped to her feet, feeling horribly sick. She reached the cloakroom only just in time and when she left it she was drenched in perspiration. Groping for the small bottle of brandy she kept mostly for emergencies, she swallowed a little with some water and was relieved to find it steadied her. There was so much to do. How could she let Dane perhaps die—she forced herself to face the possibility—without making sure he knew about Jonathan? Her own feelings regarding

Dane weren't so easy. That she was shocked by the news she had just heard didn't really prove anything. Anyone, even those having little to do with the oil men would be. Eden didn't pause to wonder if the scale of her own shock wasn't far greater than it might have been had she been just anyone, and not cared anything for him?

Gaining strength from the brandy, she automatically set about locking up the shop and putting a notice in the window informing customers that she would be closed until the following week. How long did it take to get to the Shetlands? Would Dane be in hospital yet? Feeling she was working with frozen fingers, she fumbled with bolts and security alarms and briefly contacted the police.

The best thing to do would be to get in touch with Burford Oils. Dane worked for them and they still had offices in London. She wasn't sure that their headquarters were there but they were most likely to be dealing with their enterprise in Shetland? They should be able to tell her how to get there and exactly where to go?

The company couldn't have been more helpful. If the man she was put through to was surprised to discover Dane Sutherland had a wife, he didn't betray it. She was, in fact, the one to be surprised at the deference she was shown, which was much more than she had expected, even allowing for Dane's responsible position. Within what seemed an incredibly short time, she was flown to Scotland on a private jet and taken to the Shetlands in a huge helicopter. The offshore base, as the man in London had called it, lay on one of the remotest islands Eden had ever seen. The moonlight might be distorting the landscape but she thought it looked a place more for seals and seabirds than for human beings.

Before she left, she'd made a brief 'phone call to France. Her mother had been aghast, not about Dane's accident, but because Eden was going to him.

'You're crazy!' she cried. 'What good will it do?'

'No one's sure how ill he is but he has to know about Jonathan.'

'Why?' Irene's voice grew even sharper. 'Hasn't he forfeited every right?'

Eden wasn't prepared to argue. There were things she had to decide for herself. 'I'll give you a ring when I get back, Mother,' she promised quickly. 'Look after Jonathan for me.'

She stared down at the island and shivered. Was her mother right? Was she making a fool of herself, coming here? The years hadn't dimmed the memory of Dane's temper. He would be furious over Jonathan, and maybe, like herself, full of regrets. Had she the right to make what could be his last hours more miserable than they need be?

The stewardess bent over her attentively. 'We're nearly there, Mrs Sutherland.'

Eden nodded. She saw the girl was curious but she had no desire to talk. Since leaving London, she had become increasingly aware of some surprise and conjecture surrounding her. It startled her and aroused a little of her own curiosity that while her claim to be Dane's wife was never questioned, no one appeared to have heard of their divorce? Unless those she had spoken to were too polite to refer to it?

The company had grown since the days when Dane and she were first married. Dane had travelled all over the world then. America, Mexico, the Middle East, to name but a few of the places. He had been working his way up, a drilling engineer with much sought after expertise and ambition. Misplaced ambition, her mother had called it. As a married man, he should have settled for an office job in London, instead of wildcatting in every hellhole on earth, as her father had put it.

Nevertheless, for all she'd had more faith then they'd had, Eden was amazed by the size of the oil terminal she arrived at. If Dane was in charge of even a part of

this, he'd come a long way since those days. Her dazed
eyes noted the huge complex of accommodation and
administration buildings, lit up and clearly discernible
through the darkness as they approached them. It was
clearly an offshore base of some magnitude, but it was
an impression that scarcely registered as all her
thoughts were centred on the man who had been her
husband. She hadn't dared ask the driver who had
driven her from the heliport how he was for fear he was
in possession of news she would rather not hear.

The hospital was small and immaculate. Dane was in
one of the side wards on his own. A doctor, who
introduced himself as Bill Fraser, came forward to meet
her as she came in. He said he was sure Dane would
appreciate her coming all the way from London to see him.

'How is he?' she faltered. The doctor's eyes were
scrutinising her swiftly but she didn't care what he
thought of her. She was only interested in Dane.

'Doing very well,' Bill Fraser replied quietly. 'With
any luck he should be completely recovered within a
few days.'

Eden stared at him suspiciously. 'But they said on the
news that he was badly injured?'

'That was from the rig, where they believed he was at
first,' Bill explained patiently. 'He was badly concussed,
but apart from that and a few cuts and bruises, he
seems to have escaped anything more serious. He's
going to have an outsize headache when he wakes up
though.'

Was this a warning or something? Eden's eyes grew
confused as she continued to gaze at the young doctor
while attempting to sort herself out. If Dane wasn't
badly injured, should she try and see him? If she was
there when he regained consciousness, what reason
could she give for being here if she didn't tell him about
Jonathan? And would he want to know about Jonathan
if he was all right? He must be leading a very satisfying
life without either of them, if the evidence around her
was to be believed. He might just consider the

information that he was a father something he'd as soon have done without, after all these years?

She heard Bill Fraser asking her to come with him. 'If you'll step this way, Mrs Sutherland,' he smiled, an encouraging hand at her elbow.

That he accepted her as Dane's wife so easily, suddenly struck Eden like a blow. Was it possible there was another Mrs Sutherland whom Dane talked of so freely that his staff felt familiar with her though they might not have met her? Dane could have married again without her knowing and his real wife might not be aware yet that he'd had an accident?

Feeling completely stunned, she was just about to babble the whole sorry story to Bill Fraser when, fortunately she came to her senses and managed to stop herself in time. If there was another Mrs Sutherland, Dane would tell her soon enough, but if she confessed to Bill Fraser that there might be, he might not let her near him. And suddenly Eden knew she had to see him, if only to reassure herself that he meant nothing to her anymore. That the pain she had suffered because of their divorce and his subsequent ignoring of the letters she had written only existed in her imagination.

The starkness of the room in cool white and blues, was typical of hospital rooms the world over. The iron bedstead was too short, of course, for a man of Dane Sutherland's stature. His feet stuck over the bottom of it while his broad shoulders all but obscured his pillows. Eden blinked in horror at the bandages around his head but kept her eyes firmly fixed on them feeling suddenly that if she looked at his face she might faint.

Bill Fraser guided her gently to a chair by the side of the bed. 'You're obviously still shocked from those first reports, Mrs Sutherland, but I can assure you your husband's going to be all right. It would take a lot more than a few bruises and concussion to knock a man like Dane out permanently. He's far too tough.'

Eden nodded numbly at the hint of humour in his eyes. 'May I sit with him, please?'

'As long as you like,' the doctor consented. 'Until he comes around, anyway.'

Eden's urgent glance fixed on his face. 'How can you be certain there won't be any after effects?'

'We can't be certain but it's unlikely. We've already run tests. Try not to worry too much, there's a good girl,' he said, his eyes softening as he saw her trying to blink back tears.

'You're very kind,' she gulped.

He grinned as though that amused him. 'I'll be kinder still and send a nurse in with a cup of tea. You look as if you could do with one.'

Eden didn't want any tea. She wasn't certain she'd be able to swallow it but she managed to murmur something that sounded like thank-you.

The door closed behind him before she dared look properly at Dane and his strong face blocked out all thought of her surroundings as she studied it. The sickness in her throat threatened to become reality again as her eyes rested on his darkly hewn features.

His eyes were closed and he was very pale, which was to be expected, but apart from this she saw he had changed. The softer lines of a man in his twenties had disappeared, making him look older than his thirty-six years. His appearance was still forceful. His powerful body had always made other men seem light-weight by comparison, but she didn't care for the new iron cast to his features.

Had she anything to do with his changed appearance? She put a hand over her unevenly thudding heart and thought not. True it was she who had demanded a divorce but Dane had agreed with an alacrity that had hardly denoted reluctance on his part. And he had never tried to get her to change her mind, nor had he tried to contact her since. This could only mean he had forgotten, perhaps her very existence? He hadn't even offered alimony cheques, just a curt note saying he wouldn't deprive her parents of the pleasure of keeping her. Which had made her so determined, after Jonathan was born, that they never should.

She sighed, her eyes clinging to him. His hair was still thick and dark with a wave that defied orderly styling. Dark brows curved above eyes which though closed would be a piercing grey, and his straight, arrogant nose accented a strong jawline and firm mouth. There was nothing weak about Dane Sutherland's face but there was nothing very comforting either.

Tentatively, because he lay so still, she touched his hands. Those large, utterly masculine hands which had once had the ability to arouse her to ecstasy. She flushed painfully, not wanting to remember or to admit the feeling creeping up her arm. His right arm must have been hurt for it was bandaged above the wrist, the whiteness of the bandage contrasting oddly against the dark hairs on his brown skin.

Eden drew a sharp breath as the tremor running through her changed to a volt of electricity as his hand suddenly clenched. She found it impossible to believe he had felt something too, but she hurriedly withdrew.

The heat in her cheeks faded and she was pale again by the time her tea arrived. The nurse who brought it looked at her sharply and asked if she was all right? Eden nodded though she wasn't quite sure. She hadn't seen Dane for over six years. Was it surprising that she was overreacting?

The nurse went out again after taking Dane's pulse and giving her another close glance. No one, Eden realised again, seemed surprised that Dane had a wife, it was her appearance that was arousing curiosity. The nurse might have been recording every detail. Eden could almost hear her relating to her friends. 'Medium height, fair, a bit on the thin side, nothing spectacular.' She couldn't think what she would do if Dane had married again and another wife turned up before he came round and she could ask him. Staring at him unhappily, she almost shook with apprehension. Hastily she grabbed her tea, hoping it would bring relief, but her throat was so tight she could scarcely swallow it.

'Oh, Lord,' she whispered aloud. 'What on earth am I to do?'

Bill Fraser came in so frequently that she couldn't doubt Dane was a very important person. The tension in her head grew and in desperation she loosened her silvery gold braids, running her fingers through them until her hair fell in a gleaming cloud over her shoulders. The doctor gave her a startled glance the next time he came in, reminding her of a boy stifling a wolf-whistle. He smiled at her so warmly that she might have been tempted to confide in him if every instinct hadn't warned her not to.

He had gone for the third time when Dane opened his eyes. She had been advised that he might not recognise her immediately but it was a shock to find him looking at her as if she was a stranger. She knew she should call Bill Fraser right away but the turmoil inside her kept her glued to her seat.

For a terrible few moments, before the room obviously swung into focus and his eyes remained blankly on her face, she began to believe he had lost his memory. Then, just as she was trying to assess in horror what this might mean to him, the blankness changed to a dawning incredulity.

'What the hell are you doing here?' he rasped, without bothering to use her name.

His voice wasn't strong but she recognised the hostility in it. 'I came to see how you were,' she whispered, somewhat inanely.

'Kind of you,' he remarked sarcastically.

'How are you feeling?' she asked hoarsely.

'Like hell,' he moved his head and winced. 'You didn't answer my bloody question.'

He made no apology for his language and the hardness of his eyes, keeping her at a distance, seemed to confirm her worst fears. 'Dane,' she croaked, 'I'd better know before someone comes in, have you married again?'

'Not yet,' he snapped, after staring at her with a puzzled frown. 'I wouldn't go through that again in a hurry.'

Eden didn't stop to examine the relief flooding

through her, taking it for what she thought it was, thankfulness that another woman wouldn't be turning up and embarrassing her by claiming Dane as her husband. Quickly she jumped to her feet to go for help but the doctor was just entering.

When he saw his patient was conscious, he turned as though to ask her to leave but Dane beat him to it.

'Get her out of here, Bill,' he ordered. 'I'm not in any condition yet to entertain a wife I haven't seen since we were both a lot younger.'

Eden flushed and bent her head as she hurried past the doctor. Had Dane meant to be deliberately insulting or was he still so badly disorientated that he didn't know what he was saying? Remembering the bitterness of their last meeting, she suspected the former and all she wanted to do was to run and keep on running. She had been a fool to come here but she'd be a bigger fool to stay! Then it came to her that she hadn't told him about Jonathan and she couldn't go home until she did. It was no good putting it in a letter he might not receive and she was sick and tired of trying to live with a guilty conscience. It might mean having to wait until Dane was better but that wouldn't be long, judging from his angry expression. A man who could get furious that quickly, after what he'd been through, must still have a lot of life left in him! Bill Fraser had advised her not to say anything that might have an adverse effect so it seemed likely that she must be patient for a few more days, but once Dane knew about Jonathan she could leave immediately. She didn't feel there was the slightest danger of Dane applying for custody. What would a man do with a small son in a place like this?

Managing to avoid what looked like another doctor and some nurses, she dived into the waiting room where Bill Fraser eventually found her. He sat down opposite, for they had it to themselves, and glanced at her pale face compassionately.

'Your husband should soon recover now, Mrs Sutherland,' he said quietly.

Eden retorted with a bitterness she couldn't conceal. 'There seems no doubt of it, with his temper so unimpaired.'

'Which is a good sign, though not when one's on the receiving end of it, I agree,' he nodded drily. 'But I shouldn't take too much notice of what he was saying, if I were you. Any man who's been through what Dane's been through, is bound to be uptight when he comes round. Even to find he's still alive must have come as a bit of a shock.'

Eden trembled. 'His—mind's not affected, is it?'

Bill actually laughed. 'You wouldn't believe that if you'd heard him just now. He would be back in the office or out on the rig again if I hadn't put my foot down. And he doesn't take kindly to anyone else wielding authority.'

Relief, of a kind, cleared a little of the painful anxiety from Eden's eyes. 'Can I see him again?'

'He's asleep,' Bill didn't say how this had been achieved. 'I think it would be better if you postponed your next visit until the morning and got some sleep yourself.'

Confusingly, she wanted to plead to be allowed to stay with Dane all night but instead she forced herself to ask. 'Where can I go?'

Bill hesitated. 'Dane said to take you to his place but it's away from the main complex and you might feel happier nearer him?'

Torn between the two alternatives, Eden reluctantly chose the first. She wasn't sure why she wanted to stay with Dane, but, at the same time, she couldn't bear the thought of him wakening up and throwing her out again. And she might not get another chance to see where he lived. Tomorrow he might regret his invitation and install her in a hotel? Suddenly she had a great desire to see what kind of a house he lived in. It might help her, she decided vaguely, to discover something about the man she had been married to. When she had married Dane, she had been only eighteen and more

interested in their sex life than his character. Now she
had no desire for sex at all but she would like to know
him better.

Bill Fraser was coming off duty and insisted on
escorting her to Dane's quarters, himself. 'I've had my
orders,' he said, 'so don't argue.'

She didn't intend to. She might have protested that
he looked as tired as she felt but as he seemed to imply
Dane's word was law, at least around here, she went
with him obediently.

The house was a good way from the main camp. She
fancied they were following the coast for she could
discern the white tips of waves to their left, over land
that might be a peat bog or heather but was impossible
to tell in the dark. Bill drove fast and didn't talk much
but he did explain a little about the events leading up to
the near disaster on the rig, for which she was grateful.
Dane had, apparently, saved many lives.

The house, itself, surprised her when they reached it.
Built harshly of stone, it looked almost as uncompromising as its owner, but inside it was quite cosy.
As Bill switched on lights and opened doors, he
revealed a comfortable lounge and large kitchen. He
didn't offer to take her upstairs but he did remark that
Dane had said she wouldn't have to worry about the
bed not being aired.

She hoped he didn't notice the colour rushing to her
cheeks as she bade him a rather strangled goodnight.
He had offered to find someone to stay with her but
she'd refused. The quiet situation of the house didn't
bother her nearly as much as an over curious
companion might.

It was though, as Bill had pointed out, very different
from living in a city. It was quiet yet, funnily enough,
she became more aware of the silence than she did of
the noise and bustle of London. There the roar of the
traffic blended into the background until one didn't
notice it, but here, instead of this happening, every little
sound seemed accentuated alarmingly. There was the

high, piercing cry of a seabird, followed by the weird,
mournful howl of a dog or fox. Then came a low
growling noise that sounded an awful lot nearer.

Eden wiped a film of sweat from her brow and with a
wry grimace walked quickly into the kitchen. What did
it matter what was out there! She was really too
exhausted to feel frightened tonight. She had got to the
stage where she might not have turned a hair had the
door burst open and a whole herd of wild animals
charged in!

Suddenly realising she had been on the go for over
eighteen hours, the last few of which had been filled
with worry and a terrible dread, she knew the most
sensible thing she could do was to forget everything and
go to bed. There was a lot to think about but, in the
morning, refreshed, she hoped by a good night's sleep,
she might be able to sit down quietly and work
something out? Making herself a mug of hot milk from
a pint she found in the fridge, she put out the kitchen
light and went resolutely upstairs to bed.

CHAPTER TWO

EDEN hadn't wished to sleep in Dane's bed but as the beds in the other rooms were bare and she could find no spare blankets, she didn't seem to have any alternative. Reluctantly she crawled into it, trying to pretend it belonged to someone else. The sheets still retained the faint scent of his body and were thrown back in a crumpled heap which took a few minutes to straighten. She wondered if he had been in bed when he had received word of the trouble on the rig? It seemed likely, from the state everything was in.

Eden tossed and turned, her head beginning to ache as sleep eluded her. She tried counting sheep and even talking to herself but it didn't work. What had she to fear? she asked herself. Dane and she were divorced but not enemies. For a few days it shouldn't be impossible to be civil to each other then, when he was stronger, she would tell him about Jonathan and go. This worked for a while until the sight of him lying injured in hospital returned to haunt her and she began feeling worse than ever.

Eventually exhaustion won and her eyelids drooped. When she woke it was seven o'clock and, with a start of alarm for having slept so long, she immediately rang the hospital. As she picked up the 'phone by the side of the bed, she hoped it wasn't a special line she wasn't supposed to be using? 'This is Mrs Sutherland.' she quickly informed the woman who answered. 'Could you tell me how my husband is, this morning, please?'

The woman introduced herself hastily as Sister McLeod. 'He's much better this morning, Mrs Sutherland, though naturally still not himself.'

Eden released a painfully held breath. 'I'll call and see him later.'

'He will be looking forward to seeing you, I'm sure,'
Sister replied warmly.

Wishing she could feel as sure, Eden dressed
hurriedly. Downstairs, she made some coffee and tried
to eat a slice of toast. The kitchen had been carefully
modernised without spoiling its cosy, rural atmosphere,
but the built in ovens didn't look much used. There was
enough in the fridge to provide light snacks but Dane
obviously took his main meals elsewhere.

She had put on a clean shirt and jeans which was the
only change of clothing she had brought with her. She
hadn't really been aware of what she was stuffing in her
overnight bag and wondered why she had chosen jeans?
Tough clothes for a tough place, she decided with a
shrug and doubtful appreciation of the subconscious
instincts which must have guided her.

Running back upstairs, she tidied the bed before
braiding her hair into a thick plait which she left
hanging down her back, without realising how young it
made her look. Her skin was so good she rarely used
much make-up, apart from a little lip gloss on her wide,
soft mouth but, this morning, she was forced to use
more than usual in order to hide the ravages she blamed
on a restless night.

The sun was shining as she picked up her bag and left
the house. It wasn't as warm here as in the south but
she found the slightly salty, seaweedy air more bracing.
She was surprised at the difference daylight made. The
house, she discovered, was only about a hundred yards
from the sea and if she hadn't still felt worried over
Dane she would have been entranced by the view. It
was true, the landscape was bare and windswept but
everything looked so clean and fresh that, amazingly
perhaps for a city dweller, she took an immediate liking
to it.

She had guessed, from the time it had taken Bill
Fraser to get here, last night, that Dane lived some
distance from the oil terminal, but she hadn't realised it
was as far as it was until she began to walk.

Unfortunately she wasn't wearing the right kind of shoes and her feet were blistered long before she reached the hospital.

Bill Fraser was startled when he caught sight of her. 'You didn't walk?' he exclaimed.

'My poor feet confirm it,' she replied ruefully.

'There's plenty of transport available. I should have remembered to tell you.' He frowned.

'You have more important things to worry about,' she said soberly. 'And apart from my feet, I enjoyed the walk. I think I needed the exercise.'

'The air up here takes some beating,' he agreed with a grin. 'That's how we're all so fit and my hospital's usually empty. Now, I expect you'd like to see your husband?'

'I know it's early . . .'

'Not here, it isn't,' he shrugged. 'You can come anytime although Dane will probably be home in a few days. He was threatening to leave this morning.'

'He really is better then?'

Eden didn't realise how relief made her face glow and heightened a beauty that again had the doctor catching his breath in an entirely unethical fashion. He sighed, 'Another man might have been still knocked out but, like I said last night, Dane's tough. It might not be possible to keep him here much longer though. Unless you can talk some sense into him.'

'I doubt it,' she said drily.

'Just try and keep him calm then.' Bill dug his hands into the pockets of his white coat while the twisted quirk to his mouth said he didn't expect miracles.

Eden guessed that was really another warning not to upset him. She nodded and followed Bill wryly. He appeared to have appointed himself her guide as well as mentor for again he took her to Dane himself.

'Your wife,' he announced, opening Dane's door, his voice containing a note of envy.

Eden walked towards the bed on legs decidedly rubbery. She half expected Dane to bawl her out. He didn't but he looked no friendlier than he had done yesterday. He was lying back against his pillows and still looked ghastly although the bandage around his head had been changed for one less bulky. Last night he had been wearing neatly buttoned pyjamas. This morning the top of them was missing and his chest and arms were a mass of bruises. Eden gazed at him in horror she was too late to conceal.

'This is no place for the squeamish,' he mocked. 'I'll forgive you if you'd rather not stay.'

'May I sit down?' she asked, glancing appealingly at Bill Fraser who shrugged sympathetically but went out, leaving them alone.

'Sit down by all means,' Dane gave his permission sarcastically. 'If you're here to tell me why you're here, you may as well do it in comfort.'

Eden positioned the chair by his bedside several times before she sank on to it. She still hadn't thought of a water-tight excuse and he was in no state yet to take the truth. Bill Fraser might slay her!

'There's no hurry to talk,' she mumbled. 'I've decided to stay and have a look around.'

'For how long?'

A frown of worry creased her brow and she glanced up to meet his narrowed eyes. There was a calculating light in them but then there would be, wouldn't there? She would be wondering herself in his position. 'Probably a few days.'

He seemed aware that she would rather not talk about it but when had that ever stopped him! She waited with baited breath, gathering her resources, but he didn't press for an answer to his first question, from which she concluded he meant to bait her a little.

She was right. He appeared to relax, lying back again and crossing his strong, muscled arms over the breadth of his chest, like a man glad of anything to relieve a boredom that threatened to kill him long before any injuries.

'You intrigue me,' he drawled. 'You couldn't get rid of me fast enough, six years ago, yet as soon as I suffer a few bruises you rush to my side.'

'I didn't know it was only a few bruises, did I?'

'Ah,' he smiled cynically. 'It was given out that I was nearly at death's door, wasn't it?'

Eden's face drained of colour as she recalled the news bulletin. 'Something like that,' she mumbled. Then, with a little more spirit, 'It wasn't funny!'

'I assure you I didn't think it was either,' he retorted, so softly that she realised the situation must have been grim. 'So,' he continued thoughtfully as she swallowed, 'you dropped everything, after all this time, and raced up here. Just what did you hope to gain by it, I wonder? A death-bed reconciliation?'

'You aren't doing a crossword!' she muttered, hands clenched.

'You're pretending you haven't a clue?' he taunted sarcastically. 'Mummy and Daddy lost all their money, have they?'

'No, of course not!' She frowned, wondering what he was getting at?

'Still,' the broad shoulders lifted, 'it would have been handy having a whack of your own. Save you having to go cap in hand all the time.'

'I don't know what you're talking about,' she retorted, suddenly not sure that she wanted to.

'Did you bring your own lawyer?' he rasped. 'Or were you hoping to use mine?'

'Lawyer . . .?'

'Just a possibility,' he mused. 'You were never that subtle. I still remember how you set about getting me to marry you.'

Eden almost jumped up and fled. Grasping the chair, she prayed her hands were strong enough to keep her there. 'I didn't come here to discuss the past, Dane. And if you think I rushed all this way in order to get you to change your will, or whatever, at the—the last moment, then you're mistaken. You wouldn't recognise something like simple human compassion, would you, if it hit you!'

'It was just a thought,' he smiled. 'After all, you must admit, the options aren't that great. If you aren't after my estate, what does that leave us with, I wonder?'

If he wondered anymore, he might be in danger of adding brain damage to the rest of his injuries! 'I'm not after anything,' she said bitterly.

The grey eyes mocked. 'What would you have done if you'd found another wife holding my wilting hand?'

Again, Eden felt her cheeks grow cold. 'It didn't occur to me at the time, that you might have married again.'

'You found me so unattractive, you couldn't believe another woman would want me?'

His eyes lit with a sardonic gleam she didn't mistake for amusement. Yet she knew he was laughing at her. Women had always wanted him—they had chased him in droves, not singly. She stared at him, not underestimating the attraction of his hard-boned face, his powerful body. Painfully she gritted her teeth, guessing he would have his following here, too. 'You know that's not true,' she replied flatly.

'I haven't married again,' he stressed, 'but there are other possibilities.'

'A—a mistress?'

'Not here, anyway. And—you?'

'Me?' she babbled, not immediately catching on.

'Yes, you!' his voice hardened relentlessly, 'I haven't been watching you for the past ten minutes without coming to some interesting conclusions. Even dressed as you are,' his glance rested derisively on her jeans, 'you don't look a day older than when we first met, but there's a definite air of maturity about you that wasn't there when I left you. Sorry,' he amended drily, 'when you left me. So, who's the lucky fellow?'

'Don't you mean unlucky?' she blazed, then thought of Trevor and flushed.

She hated Dane's knowing, 'Ah . . .!' as much as the cold scorn in his eyes but, before she could reply, the door opened and two nurses marched in.

Eden hadn't heard a knock so she supposed it wasn't customary. At least no one apologised for the omission. The leading one said politely. 'I'm afraid you'll have to excuse us for a short while, Mrs Sutherland. We have things to do for your husband.'

'Couldn't she stay?' Dane asked idly. 'If she's going to be around for a while, maybe she could pick up a few tips?'

The sarcasm in his voice might be carefully concealed but it didn't escape Eden. She hoped the nurses were too preoccupied with their medical responsibilities to be over astute in other directions. She was aware of their curious glances, though, when she flushed scarlet and nearly ran from the room. Again, like the last time she had been here, she almost decided to keep on running, but again, because of Jonathan, she knew she couldn't. But when she did return, though she couldn't guarantee it would be today! she would inform that man, in no uncertain terms, that she wasn't prepared to put up with his horrible hints and innuendoes! Anymore, she vowed furiously, and she would leave, Jonathan or no Jonathan! But, if she did, would it bother him? Eden almost laughed at herself for wondering. How could it, with so many nurses fawning over him, eager to obey his slightest whim. She clenched her teeth when she thought of the privileges they were enjoying, then asked herself sharply if she had taken leave of her senses!

Fearing it might be possible, she slumped into the waiting room, trying to decide what to do next? Yesterday morning, she had at least felt relatively sane and sensible, intelligent enough to be running her own business, keeping Trevor at bay and coping with her mother. Even when she heard of Dane being in London, she'd never considered him a problem—now she did! He had her churned up inside until she scarcely knew what she was saying or doing, and the effort of trying to keep even one step ahead of him was exhausting. She wasn't sure it was only her head that was affected, either. When she had looked at him, both

last night and this morning, something had passed
between them, causing her heart to accelerate so
furiously that, if a nurse had by some chance taken her
pulse and temperature instead of Dane's, she might
have thrown her into bed beside him.

She was going hot again from the trend of her
thoughts when Bill Fraser popped his head around the
door. 'Come into my office,' he invited, 'and you can
tell me what you think of your husband, this morning?'

Eden followed him doubtfully to another small room,
so cluttered, she wondered how she could get in. 'He
seems—brighter,' she muttered.

Bill glanced at her quickly as he cleared a space for
her to sit down. 'He's recovering,' he agreed, 'but not as
fast as he thinks he is.'

From the way he was smiling at that dark eyed
nurse . . .! ran her thoughts, swiftly stemmed. Stiffly she
remarked, 'You mentioned before, he might not be
willing to stay long?'

Pouring two cups of coffee from a bubbling
percolator, Bill pushed one of them towards Eden,
along with cream and sugar. 'This is what I've been
thinking about while you've been in seeing him. In a
day or two, maybe sooner, he's going to be demanding
to be out and, as I said earlier, we won't have ropes
strong enough to tie him to his bed.'

'So?' she glanced at him in unconscious urgency, in
what she felt was a pregnant pause.

Bill hesitated but only for a moment. 'I don't know if
you have a job, Mrs Sutherland, and you probably
think it cheek that I should ask whether you have a job
or other ties in London, but I wouldn't allow Dane to
go home unless you'd consent to stay and look after
him?'

'For how long?' She didn't realise she was asking the
same question that Dane had asked her.

'A week, perhaps,' he replied cautiously. 'I don't
suggest we can keep him out of action that long but if I
felt I had someone I could rely on to keep a general eye

on him and report anything doubtful to me, I'd be a lot happier.'

'Doubtful?'

'Bad headaches, exhaustion, that kind of thing, such as only someone actually living with him might be aware of. Anything that seems to be bothering him. I'm not being entirely unobjective, Mrs Sutherland,' he confessed, drily. 'Your husband is a very important man and a lot of people, including myself, rely on him for a living.'

'No one's irreplaceable,' she frowned.

'Some of us aren't,' he replied enigmatically.

The doctor was waiting for her to agree to his request. She knew this yet still hesitated. All her instincts were warning her to refuse yet she felt very tempted. 'The islands are very wild and isolated,' she floundered, as the war inside her grew fiercer and her confusion increased.

'That's not the point,' Bill retorted impatiently, then murmured a brief apology. 'Sorry, I realise you may have problems. Anyway,' he smiled, 'you can always think it over and let me know.'

Eden nodded and thanked him for the coffee. 'I have an antique shop in London,' she confessed, 'which I run single-handed. I'm not sure I can leave it. I'd have to consider.'

'Do that,' he glanced at her keenly. 'You're still far too pale. Why don't you go and get some fresh air while you're thinking about it and I'll see you later?'

'W-what about Dane?' she asked uncertainly. 'We were . . . er . . . talking.'

'I should leave him to rest, if I were you,' Bill advised with a grin. 'If he accuses you of neglect, I'll take full responsibility.'

It was a relief to give in. To have a legitimate excuse, at least for a time, to escape Dane's mockery. Yet, while she had to think about what Bill Fraser had asked her to do, she knew there were things she must clarify with Dane before she could agree to anything. Bill's request had shaken her. It might not be impossible to stay here longer than she had intended but if she was forced to look after Dane in the intimacy of his own home, she couldn't pretend it would be easy.

Outside, she was startled when a heavy man in his early forties, jumped from a sturdy looking vehicle and saluted her smartly.

'Mr Sutherland's driver, Sandy Brown, ma'am, at your service, with instructions to take you anywhere you wish.'

'Whose instructions?'

'Doc Fraser's, ma'am, but I know the boss would just about boil me in oil if I didn't look after his missus, beg pardon, ma'am, his wife.'

Eden smiled to put him at ease but still felt rather surprised. 'Thank you,' she said. 'You're very kind. Where do you come from?'

'London, same as yourself.'

She wondered where he'd got that information from? He beamed and was burly, reminding her of Briggs, who had always been her friend. She decided to accept his offer of help. 'I was going to try and find somewhere to have an early lunch but if you'd drop me off at the nearest shoe shop, I'd be grateful.'

That Brown was far quicker witted than he looked was evident when he followed her line of thinking exactly. Glancing at her three inch heels, he nodded understandingly and, being a man of action, rather than words, in no time at all Eden found herself standing outside a small shoe shop cum haberdashery, watching Brown depart after arranging to pick her up from the hospital afterwards. Even with flat heels, she didn't think she could face the long walk to Dane's house again that day, always supposing he allowed her to return there?

The shop offered a far greater choice than Eden had expected and she quickly selected a pair of sturdy shoes and sensible sandals. She noticed, on her way to the hotel Brown had recommended, that there were several other shops selling a variety of things.

The lunch served by the hotel was so substantial that she doubted she would need any supper. She had to refuse the sweet trolley and cheese and only had coffee because it provided an excuse to linger in the very comfortable dining-room to do some thinking, which she felt she must do, before she returned to the hospital.

She thought of Bill Fraser's request. It would provide her with a feasible excuse for staying, if she agreed to look after Dane, but she shrank from the ensuing intimacy. She had no fear that he would make any demands on her, he was too ill for one thing, but she couldn't dismiss a niggling suspicion that she might not be as indifferent to him as she thought she was. It would be disastrous if she discovered her old feelings for him hadn't died and when she went back to London she had to start the difficult task of forgetting him all over again.

Yet, if she refused to look after him what excuse could she give for hanging around until he was strong enough to know about Jonathan? It seemed she had no choice but to do as Bill Fraser asked. Only she must make sure that Dane got the impression that she would have done the same for anyone, under similar circumstances.

When she finally left the hotel, she wandered about the town for a while. It intrigued her, with its narrow streets and inviting alleyways, begging to be explored. They offered a sense of tranquility she knew she wouldn't find with Dane. She had to almost force her footsteps away from them to return to him.

At the hospital she was taken to his room, this time by the dark-eyed nurse. She had black hair and blue eyes and didn't seem very friendly. As they arrived at his door, Eden said she could see herself in and watched the girl depart with a flounce that made her curious.

As soon as she went in, Dane launched straight into the attack, as though he was in a bad mood and looking for someone to take it out on.

'You must have grown a thinner skin since I knew

you,' he remarked caustically as she sat down. 'Been licking your wounds, have you? I'd began to think you weren't coming back.'

'I may not have done if I'd known I was going to be welcomed by insults,' she snapped.

His dark brows lifted derisively. 'You can't expect me to be full of charitable feelings.'

'We probably both made mistakes,' she admitted, easing out of her jacket then wishing she had left it on as his eyes followed the taut movements of her body.

'I did when I married you,' he drawled.

'One more crack like that!' she cried, flushing angrily and jumping to her feet.

'Sorry!' he apologised. 'Sit down, I won't mention it again.'

She obeyed, without intending to, which made her even more furious. 'You'd better not!' she muttered tersely.

'So . . .' he began, after a long pause during which Eden tried to control her conflicting emotions, 'where were we, when we were so ruthlessly torn apart a few hours ago?'

'You don't have to pretend you weren't delighted,' she retorted coldly. 'I saw how you looked at that dark-eyed nurse . . .'

He smiled at her tauntingly. 'I was only showing a little appreciation.'

'I expect she's well paid?'

'So are a lot of people,' he retorted blandly, 'but they're not all as willing as she is.'

'I bet!'

'You can't be jealous?'

Refusing to believe it, Eden glared at him then subsided. 'No, of course not.' Defiantly she rejected this as the cause of another wave of anger tearing through her. 'It must be this unusual situation.'

He stared at her speculatively for a further moment, then, appearing to accept this, he said smoothly. 'Well, let's get back to where we left off.'

Eden frowned in alarm. He had been asking questions about her love life, which she didn't want to talk about as it was practically non-existent. 'Dane,' she broke in hastily, 'since last night I've been trying to ask you something but you've either distracted me yourself or someone else has interrupted.' Pausing, she drew a taut breath. 'You've obviously mentioned you were married as no one seemed surprised when I turned up, but does anyone know we're divorced?'

'Not that I'm aware of,' he retorted silkily. 'I'm safer with an estranged wife. As a divorced man I'd be a target for all sorts of things.'

'Such as husband hunting women?'

'Some get desperate.'

'Still, it must be nice to be even that popular,' she remarked acidly.

'You'd rather I wasn't?' he asked idly.

She hated the hint of satisfaction in his eyes which she couldn't account for. Her own eyes, a softer, more cloudy grey than his, with a touch of violet in them, sparkled. 'Your popularity rating with the opposite sex doesn't interest me. I just want to know where I stand, that's all.'

'My popularity rating doesn't absorb me either,' he returned sardonically, his eyes narrowed on her face as if trying to do a teleprint of her mind. 'What does, is what lies behind your motives in coming here. This morning we ruled out a deathbed reconciliation or a change of will. So what do we have left?'

'No doubt it will keep you amused trying to guess,' she flung back, then could have bitten her tongue out. She had as good as admitted there was a reason. Now he wouldn't rest until he got it out of her. And, once he began putting pressure on, however would she be able to keep her secret from him?

She was so startled when he didn't begin immediately that her eyes rounded when he let the subject drop and merely asked if she liked his house?

'Yes, I do!' Her pale face lit up, 'I like it very much,'

she replied enthusiastically, 'especially the situation. It was dark, last night, and I couldn't see properly but, this morning, I thought it was wonderful.'

'Everyone does,' he said drily, 'until the first hint of bad weather.'

She refused to let him spoil her pleasure. 'I suppose the weather can be drastic but I've always liked storms.'

'I remember.'

He wasn't talking of the weather now, but of the way they had fought. She flushed but refused to admit she realised. 'Anyway,' she plunged, as a lead up to what was important, 'I was wondering if you'd object to my staying there a few more days? I could do with a short holiday and, since you'd be here,' she gestured rather distractedly around the room.

His eyes glittered derisively. 'You mean you'd like to stay in my house and sleep in my bed, as long as I'm not in it?'

The colour in her cheeks deepened as her eyes slid away from his and she tried not to think of her restless loneliness. 'You have other beds,' she said sharply. 'I was merely trying to point out that I wouldn't be in your way.'

'What if I were to inform you that I don't intend remaining here more than another twenty-four hours? I might even cut it down to twelve.'

She wished he would stop rubbing a hand over the rough hairs on his chest. It was distracting and her palms tingled as they seemed to remember it was a privilege they had once enjoyed. Briefly she closed her eyes but not before she caught the sardonic glitter in his. 'You aren't fit enough to leave hospital yet.'

'Matter of opinion,' he sounded as if it was an argument he was tired of hearing. 'One thing's for sure, no man ever gained anything by lying on his back. Women might.'

Eden ignored how her heart leapt. She had threatened before but one more gibe like that and she really would walk out! Bill Fraser would have to look for someone else to look after his patient!

She glanced up to find Dane laughing at her, as though he could read her thoughts. 'Your mother once called me a rough, insensitive oil man.'

'You don't have to deliberately promote the image!' she returned to the attack. 'Your doctor wouldn't allow you to go back to—what do you call your house?'

'Sea View,' his mouth quirked.

'On your own.'

'Perhaps he could spare me a nurse for a few days?' his eyes gleamed as if he was pleased with the idea. 'The dark-eyed one?'

Eden flinched. She hadn't thought of this. 'You'd want me to leave?'

'There are good hotels,' he appeared to consider. 'Two women, you see, in the same house, fighting over me.'

Icily she met his eyes. 'I wouldn't.'

'I thought not.'

Confused, she mumbled. 'Bill Fraser says . . .'

'A damn sight too much, if I'm any judge!' Dane cut in harshly. 'Do you honestly believe I'm not on to his little game? I've seen the way he looks at you and if he tells me once more how sweet you are, I'll punch his face in! If he imagines he's going to keep me here while the pair of you play games in my bed, then he can think again!'

'I've only just met him!' she retorted, insensed. 'And Bill Fraser's not like that.'

'All men are like that, you little fool!'

'Well, I'm not!' she shouted back.

The sudden silence in the room could have been cut with a knife as they glared at each other. She saw his hands and jaw clench as he fought for control. 'All right,' he muttered, as she grew panic-stricken, believing she had upset him and might have done irreparable damage, 'Let's calm down. I'm only trying to point out that both Fraser and I have positions to maintain.'

She tried to make a similar effort though she guessed, that for some reason, he had sounded deliberately pompous. 'You appear to have a very high position? In fact, I've been curious about it. When we were married . . .'

'I didn't have enough ambition, at least not in the right direction.'

'I never said that . . .'

'Maybe it was your parents who did,' he allowed, 'but you agreed with them.'

Eden frowned. 'I didn't do that either. Well,' she faltered at the scornful glint in his eye, 'not exactly, but I had always been guided by them. It wasn't as easy to stop thinking their way as I'd believed it would be.'

'Marrying me took about all the opposition you were capable of,' he mused. 'Afterwards you found it easier to give in and you thought I would. Like a spoiled child, you didn't really wish to change.'

'Can't we get back to what we were talking about?' she pleaded tautly, knowing he might be near the truth but still resentful that he hadn't understood her better. Her parents had kept on saying it until she had really begun to believe she was a neglected wife and Dane had done nothing to correct the impression by being almost constantly away.

'Sure,' he agreed carelessly, beginning to look tired. 'At least we can always recap. You wish to act the caring little wife for a few days. Well, why not? It may be interesting to find out how much we've both changed?'

'Perhaps we haven't?' she said bleakly.

'Six years is bound to make a difference,' he mocked. 'We could discover things about each other we've never known before.'

Her clear skin flushed as she thought of Jonathan. She didn't want to dwell on what Dane might think when he discovered about him! Quickly she changed the subject. 'If you're to be allowed out tomorrow, though you'd be wiser not to count on it,' she warned, 'I'll have to get the house ready for you.'

'I've only been gone a couple of days,' he said drily.

'You don't seem to have much food in?'

'There's a freezer in the utility,' he told her briefly, 'which Brown keeps well stocked. I don't know why as I usually eat out but there's probably enough there to feed an army. You've met Brown, I take it?'

'Yes,' she realised Dane must have checked. 'This morning. I like him. He's very obliging and reminds me of Briggs.'

'Ah, yes. Your father's general factotum,' he murmured drily. 'Would your father have liked me better if I'd had Brown in those days, do you think?'

Wishing she had never mentioned Briggs, Eden felt no happier when Dane asked suavely, 'How are your parents, by the way?'

'Very well.' She forced herself to add, 'They're in France at the moment.'

'Why aren't you with them?'

'I haven't been there since—our honeymoon,' she replied stiffly.

'That should tell me something,' he taunted thoughtfully, 'if only how much you hate me?'

'I don't hate you,' she whispered, feeling the words torn from her.

'Prove it,' he muttered, his hand snaking to her wrist as she jumped to her feet in panic, making it impossible to escape.

'I'll see you tomorrow,' she croaked.

'Eden!'

Somehow her eyes were locked with his and she couldn't look away. The pupils of his were becoming fixed and hot, while her own felt distended. A dazed feeling was creeping over her and her nerves began to tingle. They stared at each other as if they'd just met for the first time and all the old breathlessness was there. Her body burned with remembered emotions as her lungs gasped desperately for air.

She tried to say something, anything to break the spell of enchantment she couldn't believe still existed, but her lips refused to move and he beat her to it.

'Kiss me, Eden,' he said thickly.

Eden, still feeling she was floating in space, was hypnotised into obeying. Slowly, as his fingers tightened on her wrist, she bent over him, lowering her head, her eyes wide open on his, receiving the impression, as his smouldered, that she was plunging into a cauldron of flames.

Her mouth went dry with anticipation and she knew she was trembling as he suddenly hooked an arm around her neck, pulling her impatiently down to him. Only then did her eyes close as he took his kiss with a hunger that almost shattered her completely. If the door hadn't opened to admit Bill Fraser, she dreaded to think what might have happened.

CHAPTER THREE

EDEN switched off the downstairs lights as she prepared to retire for the second night she was about to spend in Dane's house. She felt exhausted for it had been a long day and she had spent the last few hours getting the house ready for his possible return in the morning.

Brown, who had driven her there at five o'clock, had told her that Dane had a woman who came in and cleaned occasionally but was away on the mainland at present. Eden didn't mind. She would rather manage on her own. This way she might be able to pay for her keep so that Dane couldn't accuse her of taking advantage of his hospitality when she left, next week.

It would have to be next week, at the latest, she decided. Even for that short time it would be a strain trying to hide the information that might turn the tolerant dislike he had for her into a very real hatred.

She had stripped his bed, putting the soiled sheets in the laundry basket to wash in the morning. Brown had shown her the cupboard where the clean linen was kept and she made up Dane's bed again and the smaller one, next door, for herself. She had worked until she could go on no longer, trying to forget how she had felt when he had kissed her, but not even under the shower, where she had stayed until almost drowning herself, had she been able to.

As she stumbled into bed, having gone down again after leaving the bathroom to find a book she knew she wouldn't read, she felt more bewildered than ever. She wasn't ready yet to admit she still loved Dane Sutherland, but even to suspect she had some feelings for him was alarming. Having believed all her love for him had died, it threw her into a panic to discover she might be mistaken.

If he could still make her pulse race after six years, how could she have given up on their marriage so easily? Dane blamed her for the divorce, or pretended to—she had certainly been the one to ask for one, but had she ever really wanted it? Restlessly she tossed under her sheets, the discarded paperback falling unheeded to the floor. They had quarrelled, saying unforgivable things to each other, but, because it had hurt so much even to think of it, she had never allowed herself to review their relationship from the beginning. Their first meeting, and its far from happy outcome, had been pushed to the back of her mind, like a bomb that might explode if given an airing. Now she was suddenly aware that she must think about it. It might be painful but she knew that somehow, she must feel reassured that the responsibility for the failure of their marriage hadn't been hers alone!

It wasn't as difficult as she had thought it might be. As soon as she relaxed and her eyes closed, she was back again in Cairo, where Dane and she had first met. With her parents she had been attending a party, a glittering affair to which the whole world and his wife appeared to have been invited. Richard Spencer, as a leading financier, was asked everywhere, but if his wife hadn't insisted, he would have turned down most of the invitations he received.

Eden had been trying to dodge the attentions of a persistent Arab sheikh, whom half the other women there were chasing, when she literally bumped into Dane. Because he looked imposing enough to discourage anyone, she grasped his arm, whispering impulsively, 'Oh, please! would you mind pretending I'm with you? Just for a moment.'

He took in the situation at a glance and acted as swiftly, which seemed to confirm her snap judgment regarding his intelligence. The next instant, she was caught in his arms and he was whirling her away from her ardent pursuer.

'How was that?' he asked gravely.

'W-wonderful,' she stammered breathlessly, then giggled, on glancing up and seeing he was laughing at her. 'I really am grateful.'

'I like being useful,' he grinned.

'I'm glad it was you,' she said simply, feeling an immediate if surprising sense of compatibility. Somehow, in his arms, she felt marvellously at ease with him, a feeling she had never experienced with any man before. She knew plenty of boys but had never been impressed by them and they all paled into insignificance beside a man like this. For a while they danced in silence then he led her to the bar and got her a drink.

As he placed something that looked suspiciously like lemonade in her hands, the humour died from his face as he studied her closely. 'You're very young to be having to fend for yourself,' he remarked.

Her eager eyes shadowed with disappointment. She was wearing a new strappy dress that revealed a lot of her slender but enticingly curvaceous figure. The oil sheikh's eyes had almost eaten her up when he'd looked at her and she didn't care for this man's disapproval. He talked as though she was just out of the schoolroom.

'My parents are around somewhere,' she admitted reluctantly, adding defiantly, 'unfortunately.'

He took a slosh of his whisky and she watched the movement of his strong throat. 'Not having a good night, are you?' he mocked, setting his glass down sharply. 'Having to dodge both parents and would-be seducers.'

The word seducer made her feel very grown-up, so she forgave him. 'Usually I'm quite able to look after myself,' she retorted haughtily.

'How old are you?' he asked abruptly.

'Eighteen,' she snapped. 'And you?'

He didn't seem to mind her tit-for-tat. 'Thirty,' he replied grimly, 'Or as near as makes no difference.'

She looked at him, then, really looked at him for the first time and believed it. He was tall and dark and would have been handsome had his features not been so strongly moulded. Every feature of his face was dominant, from his thick brows to the fiercely grey eyes and harshly sculpted mouth. His jaw and chin might have been chiselled. Altogether, with a body that appeared to be comprised of whipcord and steel, he was a very formidable looking individual.

'You do pick them!' her friend Sherry teased in a cloakroom, later. 'Who is he? What does he do?'

'An oil man from the Gulf,' Eden replied cautiously.

'Lucky you!' Sherry exclaimed enviously.

'Invite me to your place, tomorrow,' Eden begged hastily, as the door opened to admit her mother. 'He wants to take me on the river.'

The river happened to be the Nile and, because Dane knew it so well, they spent an idyllic afternoon and evening. Eden's parents, believing she was enjoying herself at the house of titled acquaintances, were too busy attending to their own affairs to wonder what it was about the Marchant's sedate establishment that was bringing such an expression of bliss to their daughter's face?

During the following days, Dane Sutherland escorted Eden all over the place. She wasn't sure why he took her out so frequently for he usually treated her as he might have done a pest of a younger sister. Nevertheless, despite an obvious hint of self-mockery, he continued to see her.

'My leave's running out,' he announced abruptly, at the end of an evening they'd spent dancing together.

'And we're going back to London,' she sighed.

'I'll be there myself in a few weeks.' His eyes darkened in the taxi that was bearing them towards her parent's hotel. 'But I don't think I'll be seeing you again, Eden.'

She was overcome by a sense of loss. The world might have collapsed at her feet! 'But you have to see me again!' she cried, staring at him in bewilderment.

'No!' he repeated firmly.

She went white. 'You can't be so cruel,' she whispered revealingly.

'Don't be such a little fool!' he retorted tersely. 'I'm a penniless oil man. Sure, I make money, but I spend it as fast.'

'W-what on?' she gulped.

His broad shoulders lifted cynically. 'What do you think? Women—drink.'

She hadn't seen him drinking that much. She suspected he was trying to put her off. 'I don't care how poor you are or how many women you've had,' she cried recklessly. 'We have to see each other again. You know that . . .'

'Eden!'

She wasn't listening. Flinging herself into his arms, she pressed her trembling lips to his. They hadn't kissed before. Because he hadn't tried to kiss her, she'd been vaguely disappointed, even impatient, but just to be near him had been enough until now. She was determined she wasn't going to be cast aside without at least knowing once what it felt like to be in his arms. But when they suddenly closed and tightened around her, hurting her almost as much as the ruthless, passionate pressure of his mouth, she was overwhelmed by the severity of what seemed like a thousand electric shocks running through her.

At this point, Eden shuddered and opened her eyes, feeling in as much of a turmoil as she had done that evening in the taxi, when Dane had finally released her. Rubbing a shaking hand over her brow, she found it damp with perspiration. She knew she needed a respite but her mind seemed like a film projector that insisted on rolling on relentlessly.

After that shattering kiss in Cairo, Dane had agreed to meet her in London. He had promised to get in touch as soon as he returned, but he didn't. That they had met again at another party had been sheer coincidence.

Eden had, in fact, been in two minds about going

Since Cairo, she seemed to have no enthusiasm left for the gay parties and late nights she had previously indulged in, and when Dane didn't turn up she became depressed. If she hadn't suddenly felt desperately that she must do something to cheer herself up, she might not have gone out that evening at all.

Strangely, too, she had just been on the point of leaving the party when Dane had arrived. He'd been with a glamorous redhead whom he'd swiftly introduced to another man when he caught sight of Eden.

'I thought I could resist you but I can't,' he groaned, holding her close after taking her home.

'You promised to give me a ring,' she reproached, her arms around his neck.

'I didn't think it was sensible to see you again. I still don't,' he replied grimly.

'Why not?'

His mouth tightened as if she shouldn't have needed to ask. 'You're far too young for an affair and what can I offer compared with that?'

That, was the beautiful house belonging to Eden's parents, they were parked outside, set in one of the most expensive commuter belts around London.

'I'm not responsible for what my parents have,' she retorted. 'I believe once, Daddy didn't have very much.'

'You're used to a life of luxury.'

Eden didn't want to talk about it. How she lived was surely unimportant. 'How long are you here for?' she asked urgently.

'Two weeks but, later, I'll be back for a month.'

Eden made the most of those two weeks even though Dane restricted himself to a goodnight kiss and firmly resisted her overtures to be more than friends. Until nearly the end.

He had a small flat in a seedy area of Holborn but it was all he required as he was so seldom there. The shabbiness was a novelty to Eden, who was used to the best of everything. She liked to pretend she was an ordinary housewife trying her hand out at cooking and dusting but there wasn't much to do. Dane usually took her out for meals and he was so seldom at the flat that it never really got untidy. What Eden enjoyed most was coming back there after dinner, making coffee and playing records and waiting for his goodnight kiss. He kept it light but she sensed triumphantly that he didn't always find it easy. As for herself, he absorbed all her thoughts; even during the night she dreamed of him continually. She loved him passionately and was certain, if he rejected her, she would never love anyone again as she loved Dane Sutherland.

'Why don't we get married?' she asked one evening, after he had held her tightly in his arms then thrust her firmly away from him. His principles were showing, she knew that, and it riled her that he should be so strait-laced with her while he might have taken another woman to bed. He wanted her and, because neither of them wanted an affair, she had no compunction about proposing. She believed he thought her about as attainable as the moon or stars and if it was left to him they might simply drift apart.

'There's nothing to stop us getting married, is there?' she persisted, as he stared at her, a startled expression in his eyes. She could tell he didn't intend encouraging the idea.

'Don't be foolish, Eden,' he replied curtly. 'I haven't time for marriage. I'd make a lousy husband, anyway, and I can't see your parents welcoming me as a son-in-law.'

Eden didn't see why not but that didn't worry her unduly. 'You wouldn't be marrying my parents,' she pointed out impatiently.

'I could be,' he observed drily. 'You've been used to living in style. You may think this is fun,' he glanced expressively around the shabby lounge, 'but you would soon change your mind if you had to live here permanently.'

'I'm young enough to adapt,' she retorted sharply.

'That's another thing,' he rapped, pouncing on her

age like he was grabbing at a lifeline. 'You're far too young for me.'

'I was eighteen two weeks ago.'

'I'm nearly thirty,' he retorted grimly. 'The age gap wouldn't have mattered but I've been around and you haven't. Despite the emancipation you're so often on about, you've led a very sheltered life, Eden. Besides, I wouldn't know what to do with a wife. I shouldn't have time to give you all the attention you'd be constantly demanding. The next few years could be crucial for me. If I'm to get anywhere it's got to be now. I couldn't concentrate on what I have in mind with a wife and maybe a couple of kids to worry about.'

'Work's not everything!' Eden countered desperately.

'No, it isn't.' His brows rose on a quirk of irony, 'But it's the only way I know to earn the kind of money I'm going to need, especially if I'm to marry a girl like you—eventually. I have to be ambitious.'

Eden was suddenly radiant. 'You do want to marry me . . .?'

'Maybe in ten years time.'

Her face fell. 'You can't expect me to wait as long as that!'

His voice hardened. 'It was you who brought it up, remember?'

'Proposed, you mean,' she glared at him.

'Let's not quarrel, sweetheart.' Taking her in his arms, he kissed her gently. 'It's just not on,' his mouth slid to her throat as he added thickly, 'not practical.'

'Why did you try and see me again if you weren't serious?' she whirled away from him in a temper. 'You encouraged me!' she cried unfairly.

'I tried not to see you again,' he reminded her, his eyes still dark from their last kiss.

'Oh, take me home!' she retorted sarcastically. 'I didn't realise you'd decided not to fall in love. I'm the silly fool who's done that, aren't I!'

He went pale but fetched her coat without another word. The tightness of his mouth suggested his

emotions might not be as uninvolved as she thought but
he didn't refute anything she said as they left the flat.

They parted like strangers and the following evening
she went out with Trevor Lawson, vowing to forget
Dane. Let him spend the last days of his leave with
another woman! She decided not to see him again but
two nights later found her knocking on his door
feverishly.

As soon as the door opened, she was in his arms.
'Oh, God, Eden!' he groaned. 'I've missed you.'

He didn't put on the light but she could see he was
pale and hadn't shaved. 'I couldn't stay away,' she
admitted. 'It's been terrible.'

The break in her voice revealed more than words
might have done. With a choked exclamation he held
her tightly to him, seeming to drink her in like a man
who had been thirsty for days. 'It was for me, too,' he
confessed hoarsely.

Putting slender arms round his neck, she pulled his
head down. 'I'm sorry I was so silly. I don't want to
spoil what we have.'

He kissed her deeply, crushing her mouth, and she
returned his kisses wildly. Then her hands slid from his
neck, down his back, under his unbuttoned shirt,
clutching at his bare skin as the room whirled about
her. Dane hadn't kissed her like this since that last
evening in Cairo, but they weren't in Cairo now. They
were alone in his flat with the door closed and the
darkness of an early spring night falling. She clung to
him like a limpet and he wasn't able to resist her. As
their kisses deepened and their hearts pounded together,
he picked her up and carried her to the bedroom.

She felt both frightened and elated as he laid her on
the bed and came down on top of her. There was
something different about him but she was only aware
of it hazily because of the difference in herself. There
were new emotions overwhelming her, moving too
swiftly and devastatingly within her to allow her to
concentrate on what was motivating him. His kisses

were different but, as they fell on her warm, soft mouth, she returned them ardently. He had so seldom shown her passion that, like a deprived child, she couldn't get enough of it. The needs he had concealed so well until now, reached out and consumed her, making the blood sing in her veins, setting her body on fire with the drugging heat of desire until her only remaining fear was that he should suddenly get up and leave her again.

But he didn't. And she could never have described how the first touch of his fingers on her naked flesh, when he swiftly stripped them both of their clothing, sent her mind reeling into realms of ecstasy. The sensuous abrasion of his roughened hands on her taut breasts aroused her until she was clinging to him blindly. Her moans of pleasure turned to gasps as she experienced sensations she had never known before when his hands moved on to caress the sensitive areas of her stomach. She dissolved completely, yielding to his every touch as his arms tightened and he pressed her body firmly to the length of his. Her eyes closed as his mouth returned to hers passionately and she felt the urgency of his increasing desire. She thought she had reached the very pinnacle of bliss even before he thrust a shaking hand under her hips and took her with a kind of savage tenderness.

The following moments left her gasping with pleasure as a new world enfolded, making her realise just how naïve she had been to imagine she had already reached it. And with the eventual flood of overwhelming sensation came the new and rather frightening awareness of the sensual capabilities of her now awakened body.

Dane didn't speak for a little while after the waves of rapture had subsided. Then he asked tersely if she still wished to marry him?

'More than ever!' Eden remembered herself choking eagerly, as if it had been yesterday.

They had gone to tell her parents. Dane hadn't met them before and she realised now that it must have been a big thing for him, meeting them and having to announce, in practically the same breath that he wished to marry their daughter. Irene had turned faint, while Richard Spencer had remarked stiffly that if this was a joke he considered it in poor taste. Their dismay, when Dane had assured them he was deadly serious, had been disconcertingly obvious.

Nevertheless, Dane had gone ahead, making arrangements for them to be married on his next leave, in three weeks' time. While her mother had wept and pleaded and her father threatened and stormed, he had listened in stony silence. Eden knew he hadn't liked being told that a penniless oil man wasn't good enough for a Spencer, or being asked how he intended keeping her? He had answered quietly enough that Eden and he would be no worse off than many other young couples, but had been adamant when it came to refusing Richard Spencer's offer of a place in his company when all other threats and cajoling failed.

Their honeymoon had been spent at St Tropez. Until then, Eden had been so excited by what she considered proof that Dane loved her, that she lived in a dream world and never stopped to wonder why he occasionally looked like a man contemplating his own funeral, rather than his wedding. Not that there had been much time for observing anything. Two days after meeting Eden's parents, he had returned to the Gulf and the day after he came back to England they were married.

During their brief honeymoon he gave up all pretence of not wanting her. He made love to her frequently but Eden soon came to perceive that though she might be his wife, she seldom occupied all his thoughts. Even in France there were continual telephone calls, from the Middle East and other places, such as New York. He had something to do with, or was contracted to Burford Oils, she had never been sure of his exact position. She hadn't been that interested. How he juggled between them and other companies was, she admitted perhaps necessary if it had to do with his work, but she only found it irritating when it interfered with their being together.

When she complained, he retorted unsympathetically, 'You knew what you were letting yourself in for.'

Indignantly she retorted. 'If you were that absorbed in your job, why did you marry me?'

'Need you ask?' he exclaimed.

'Oh,' she averted her face, cheeks burning. 'You can't mean because you seduced me?'

'Not exactly,' he mocked, eyes glinting. 'From the beginning it's been the other way around, hasn't it? But I should have known better.'

'Than to marry me?' She felt sure this was what he had been going to say. 'You don't love me?'

'Eden!' Reaching for her, he almost shook her in exasperation. 'Let's forget about that, shall we? You know damn well that I care for you.'

Eden gazed at the ceiling of Dane's house in Shetland, unhappily. That was about as far as he had ever committed himself and she had resented that, too. It added to the bitterness that had built up over the ensuing weeks, after their honeymoon in France was cut short because of Dane's work and during the odd days he had managed to see her over the following months. Usually he'd arrived unannounced and left in much the same fashion, thrusting some money into her hands and telling her to be good until he returned.

The flat had begun to suffocate her, or it may have been that it had taunted her with his absence. She had accepted the offer of a better one in Knightsbridge from her parents and left a note of the address for Dane. But when he found her he had dragged her back.

'I won't accept charity!' he had fumed. 'I can keep my own wife.'

'It's not as if you ever wanted a wife!' she had countered angrily. 'Mummy and Daddy were only trying to help. I could have gone home if I'd wished . . .'

'For good?' Dane's grey eyes had glittered.

She hadn't seen how tired he was, the lines of strain

on his face. It shook her now that she clearly recalled
he'd looked grey, yet it hadn't registered at the time.
She had only known that when he'd made passionate
love to her that night, that it was no good. She had
convinced herself that she'd tried to be a good wife,
doing everything she could to please him, but that she
couldn't be expected to put up with his indifference and
neglect any longer! He had betrayed many times, in
various ways, that their marriage was an inconvenience
he could well have done without, so it must be up to her
to end it? This she had done, the very next morning.

It had been easier than she had expected, with help
coming indirectly from another source. Trevor had
rang, demanding to know why she was slumming it
again? His voice had carried clearly as he'd reminded
her he was picking her up to take her to her parents for
lunch.

It had been a completely innocent arrangement. She
hadn't been out with Trevor since she had known Dane,
but he had refused to listen. He had been livid and even
more so, a few minutes later, when her mother rang to
ask why she was back in that, terrible place?

After that everything had blown up. They'd had the
most terrible row, culminating in Dane throwing some
things back into his case and leaving. 'You couldn't
wait to get married,' he'd rasped grimly. 'Now you
want a divorce. You still have a lot of growing up to do
and I suggest you do it before you try again. I'll see my
solicitor right away.'

He had, without even attempting a reconciliation.
Her father had done the rest. Eden frowned. Her anger
and resentment had continued far longer than it should
have done. It had been fostered, she realised now, to a
great extent by other people to whom she ought not to
have listened. Frequently she accused Jonathan of
listening to her mother but he wasn't really old enough
to know better, while she had no such excuse! Even
when she had discovered she was pregnant, she had
listened when Irene had advised her not to tell Dane.

Eden hadn't held her mother wholly responsible for this decision though. She had herself thought that, far from welcoming such news, he would merely consider it as another rope around his neck. It wasn't until it was too late, as had been proved, for a reconciliation of any kind that she had attempted to get in touch with him.

Eden lay still for a few more minutes then suddenly rolled to the side of the bed and sat up as the familiar nausea rose in her throat. Since she had been a small child, she felt sick whenever she was disturbed about something. And she was disturbed about something now. Her whole being seemed to be writhing in an agony of shame and regret. Dane had maybe been partly at fault but she had acted like a spoiled child, determined on having her own way. How could she have proposed to a man she had only known two weeks? She should have been content to wait a year or so and given them a chance to know each other better. She could have occupied herself over the career she had been considering and it would have given him time to get used to the idea of having a wife. She would have grown up, as he had suggested she needed to, while he would have done his own re-adjusting. They might have been married when she was twenty and been incredibly happy if she hadn't spoiled everything by demanding to be married straight away.

She couldn't remember exactly how she had felt when she had returned to Dane's flat, after their first quarrel, but it was no use pretending he had seduced her; she had been more than willing. But she could understand how, afterwards, he had felt trapped into marriage. Now all she had left was Jonathan and, because of her own stupidity, she might be in danger of losing him as well. At the very least, when she told Dane about him, he was going to be furious that she hadn't found some way of making sure he knew about his son before now!

Eden felt terribly ashamed of herself. There was also a sense of humiliation she hadn't previously known. Dane had obviously married her against his will. He had discovered she hadn't been to bed with anyone else and had been driven by his conscience, but the speed with which he had accepted her offer of a divorce proved that he'd considered the fault partly hers and, having done his duty was entitled to his freedom. Any day now, she might expect him to ask mockingly why she hadn't managed to inveigle another poor fool into marrying her, but if he did, wouldn't she deserve it?

Eden was pale the next morning when she got up. She had a feeling that she had tried and convicted herself during the night and the subsequent despair she felt weighed very heavily. If she had thought he would have given it, she would have rushed straight to Dane and begged his forgiveness but she realised this might achieve nothing but his contempt. There could be no forgiveness for what she had done. The most she could hope for was that he might allow her to look after him for a while, thus enabling her to make some small amends.

With this in mind, she rang the hospital but they couldn't give any definite information. 'If we can keep your husband here, Mrs Sutherland, we will. I don't think he's fit to be out yet but we'll have to see.'

Brown arrived, just as she was putting down the receiver. He had the milk. 'Shall I make you some coffee, ma'am?' He glanced at her keenly. 'You look tired.'

'That would be nice,' she smiled, pleased to see him. 'And my name's Eden. I've been worried about Dane,' she explained haltingly. 'He wants to come home and they're trying to keep him in. Who do you think's going to win?'

'Put your money on the boss, every time,' Brown grinned then sobered. 'Concussion's not to be fooled with though. It's a pity he didn't realise . . .'

'I agree,' Eden nodded drily as Brown deftly handled breakfast. 'I only hope I can look after him properly. If he has a relapse, what then? He seems to have, I mean,' hastily, 'he has a very important position with the firm.'

'Well, you could say he is the . . .' Brown began then
paused, as abruptly as Eden had in the middle of her
last sentence. 'Yes, well, he is important but I've seen
him get out of bed when he's scarcely been able to
stand.'

'Because of other accidents, you mean?'

'An oil man's life is full of them, Miss Eden, ma'am,
though thank goodness they're not all that serious.'
Brown smiled reminiscently, 'I recall . . .'

'I'd rather not hear, if you don't mind,' Eden
protested quickly. 'I . . . er . . .' She looked at him
frankly, 'You're probably aware, Brown, that Dane
and I haven't seen much of each other these last years.'

'So I believe.' Brown didn't try to hide he was aware
of this, for which Eden respected him. 'All marriages
have their ups and downs.'

Hers seemed to have been all in one direction! Eden
nodded bleakly, wishing suddenly that Dane hadn't
chosen to keep quiet about their divorce. She'd felt
grateful when he told her no one knew, now she wasn't
so sure. It might prove more of an embarrassment than
the truth might have been, in the long run?

'I have a business to run but I will be staying until
next week,' she said. 'I would like to make sure Dane is
almost completely recovered before I leave.'

Brown nodded understandingly, glancing away from
the anxiety in Eden's eyes which revealed more than she
realised. 'Anything I can do to help, Miss Eden, ma'am,
just give a shout. I'm used to Dane's ways and it would
be no trouble.'

Eden thanked him gratefully, not so foolish as to
reject such an offer which she sensed she might be glad
of, if only to get her to the airport when Dane told her
she was no longer welcome!

Demonstrating a total disregard for his doctors, Dane
came home that afternoon. When Eden had visited him in
hospital, that morning, and had added her voice to the
rest, he had merely told her cuttingly to run away and not
interfere in things which were none of her business. He

could have worded it differently, she'd thought unhappily. He refused to travel in an ambulance, either, and arrived home with Brown, looking almost as grey as the sea, beneath overcast skies.

Eden made the mistake of running out to meet him, her mane of hair flying loose about her shoulders, feet bare in sandals. She hadn't expected the blue-eyed nurse to be with him and regretted she hadn't brought a smart dress to put on as she noticed the contrast between the flattering uniform of the nursing profession and her own scruffy jeans. The nurse had her hand under Dane's arm, far too proprietorially, Eden considered, but when she offered to assist him herself, he replied curtly that he didn't need any more help.

Flushing with humiliation, Eden retreated, only partly mollified to hear the nurse routed as well, when she advised Dane to go straight to bed. He nearly snapped her head off. It was Brown who got him there, with the help of Bill Fraser, who drove up behind them.

'He doesn't need constant medical attention,' Bill said as he left, taking the nurse with him. 'But I'll be in touch all the time and if anything worries you, Mrs Sutherland, give me a ring. Somehow,' he grinned, 'for the rest of the day, I don't think he will be giving you much trouble.'

After they had gone and she went tentatively to Dane's bedroom, she thought Bill could be right. Dane was sleeping and seemed exhausted—she crept quietly to the bed, apprehensive of disturbing him. As in the hospital, when he had been unconscious, she found herself absorbing every inch of his face. Although it was as strong as ever, there were more lines on it than she could remember. There was a whiteness under his skin and he looked drained. Pity overwhelmed her, though, like then, she feared it might be misplaced.

She wasn't aware that he was looking at her from under his lashes until he opened his eyes and his brows rose. 'You find the spectacle of me lying here helpless, interesting?' he asked.

She flushed and jumped back as if stung. 'Naturally I feel concerned, if that's what you mean,' she retorted stiffly. 'But I'd never believe you were helpless.'

'You show a little more sense than you used to,' he allowed.

'If I do, it's more than you're doing, just now!' she exclaimed, her pulse jerking unevenly as he began struggling out of the top of his pyjamas. Swiftly she forced herself to help him, knowing it would be useless to continue protesting. Yet she couldn't help remarking sharply, 'You should have stayed in hospital longer. If you have a relapse, you'll only have yourself to blame.'

CHAPTER FOUR

'You always were a nagging wife.' Dane said broodingly, adding, when Eden didn't answer. 'They could do no more for me in hospital than you can do here. And after all you offered,' he smiled silkily. 'I suffered no damage to speak of, apart from the knock on my head, which is really nothing to make a fuss about. All I need is time.'

'Which I hope you're going to give yourself,' she replied coldly. 'You must realise how ill you've been.'

Ignoring this with a frown, he countered abruptly. 'Are you any good at secretarial work?'

'Not really,' she frowned, 'I can do bookkeeping, after a fashion . . .'

He stared at her narrowly. 'That sounds interesting. Don't tell me you're usefully employed?'

Eden tried not to notice the derision and answered evasively, 'I hadn't time to do anything before we were married.'

Apparently diverted. he rubbed a hand over his brow. 'Ours must have been one of the shortest marriages on record.'

She walked away from him to the window, her hands clenching nervously. 'I don't think we were ready for marriage, either of us. I was young and foolish and you were too preoccupied in other directions.'

'You could be right.' He shot her a grim glance which she felt right down her spine, 'We certainly made a hash of it.'

'Yes,' she agreed dully, hoping he didn't see her wince.

'At least you had the sense to realise it would never work,' he shrugged, as she turned around again. His grey eyes had something in them she couldn't quite make out as his glance swept over her slowly, 'Though anyone, looking at you, might be right in thinking I should have had my brains examined for letting you go.'

A compliment? She thought not. 'You wouldn't agree though?'

'I regretted one side of our relationship,' he conceded. 'You were wonderful in bed.'

'If that's all . . .' she began hotly, then stopped short as he lay back with a groan. Oh, God, what was she thinking about? She had been left in charge of him—she was supposed to be looking after him. No wonder the dark-eyed nurse had looked at her so scathingly! While Dane was growing exhausted she was allowing a quarrel to develop that wasn't doing him any good. 'Dane, I'm sorry,' she said remorsefully. 'Can I get you anything?'

'A drink?'

'Tea?'

'No!' His voice was briefly stronger. 'You'll find some whisky downstairs.'

Would Bill Fraser approve? She hesitated but he was so pale that she gave in but fetched him only a small one. 'I'll bring you some tea as well,' she said anxiously. 'Then you must rest.'

'What do you think I've been doing the last few days?' his mouth thinned as he studied the thimbleful of whisky and he swallowed it at one go. She wondered if he was punishing her for being so niggardly over his drink when he said coolly. 'By the way, when my secretary arrives, would you please let her in?'

Eden stared at him suspiciously, her eyes wide with alarm. He couldn't have used the 'phone? She had only been gone a minute. 'Bill Fraser wouldn't approve.'

'I've a business to run,' Dane replied curtly.

'But you're ill!' she cried desperately. 'I've told you before, you could have a relapse.'

'More than likely,' he agreed indifferently. 'I'll probably have a few before I'm completely well again. You all expect it and can't all be wrong.'

'We're only trying to help,' she retorted.

'I might appreciate your help better if you tried holding my hand and soothing my fevered brow,' he suggested sarcastically, 'instead of nagging.'

There was a loud knock on the door before Eden could explode. 'That will be Brown, now, with Miss Petrie,' he exclaimed.

Eden tried to count ten but didn't make it. 'Do I bring her up?' she asked, quietly seething. Wait until she got on the 'phone to Bill Fraser—and wouldn't she tell Brown a thing or two!

'No need, she knows the way,' Dane replied suavely, raising Eden's blood pressure again as she realised what that implied.

'How many women have you had in your bed?' she said scornfully, as the door opened to admit an iron-grey lady of indisputable respectability. She was middle-aged and plain though very elegant in faultless tweeds which didn't appear to affect her cool demeanour, though the sun, outside, was very hot. Eden shuddered to think what Miss Petrie would have thought, could she have overheard her last remark and guessed what she'd implied.

Dane, a glint of revealing laughter in his eyes as he relished her discomfort, made the introductions. As Eden shook his secretary's hand, he said glibly. 'I won't keep you long, Edith. I want to see Kildare.'

'He's on his way, sir.' Miss Petrie, notebook at the ready, pencil poised, sat down obligingly in the chair Eden pushed weakly towards her. 'You must understand, sir, that everything's been taken care of. Thanks to your prompt action, the damage on the rig was minimal. Everyone is . . .'

'That's enough, Edith.' He jerked upright, winced, but maintained his position, once achieved. 'I didn't bring you here to gild my halo. You know as well as I do that what I did was all in the day's work. Eden, could you bring Miss Petrie a cup of tea, please? She prefers it to coffee.'

Still angry, Eden obeyed. She didn't need to be told, as his eyes sharpened on the bulky folder Miss Petrie was carrying, that it was his way of getting rid of her. After taking Miss Petrie her tea, she retreated to the kitchen and closed the door, but she would have had to be deaf not to have heard the steady tramp of personnel entering and leaving the house throughout the entire afternoon. Eventually, believing that Dane could be inviting a setback far worse than ever he imagined, she took advantage in a lull in the comings and goings to firmly lock and bolt the door, shouting fiercely through the letter box to the next caller that Mr Sutherland wasn't seeing anyone else today!

'Not even me?' replied an amused voice.

It was Bill Fraser. Thankfully she let him in. 'About time, too!' she muttered sharply, locking the door again.

'I got your message,' he apologised wryly. 'But we had an emergency appendicitis case and there was no one to spare. I came as soon as I could.'

'I realised something must be holding you up,' she smiled wearily.

He glanced keenly at her flushed cheeks. 'So he's had half the staff here, has he? Only to be expected, you know.'

'You shouldn't allow it.'

'If I'd tried to stop it, it might only have made things worse. Brown was on to me as well,' he said drily, 'but I knew it was no use coming until he was down to his last breath.'

'You should see how he looks.'

'I don't need to see, I can guess. I'll give him something to put him out for the rest of the night and tomorrow I may be able to talk some sense into him.'

The following day Eden wasn't sure what Bill had said to convince Dane he wasn't superhuman, but no one came to the house, nor did he demand to see anyone.

Eden was glad of the respite though he kept her

running up and downstairs continually. He proved to be a terrible invalid, full of complaints and forever trying to get out of bed and, because she hadn't had any experience of nursing anyone before, she found it very heavy going. Yet, despite the question of Jonathan at the back of her mind, she found herself suddenly absorbed in rediscovering her husband. She realised Dane wasn't her husband now but somehow this didn't seem important. A new excitement was growing inside her. Getting to know him again seemed an even greater adventure than it had been the first time. As the days progressed, she found herself increasingly drawn to him, no matter how much he shouted and complained, and it came to her slowly that she must still have some feelings left for him. That some of the love she had felt for him must still be there.

The third day after his return he began getting up more and perhaps because she was wary that he could still make her heart race, she regretted the lack of locks on the inside doors when she found him in her bedroom one morning. She stood staring at him speechlessly. He couldn't find anything she didn't wish him to see but the implied intimacy disturbed her.

'Come in,' he drawled coolly. He had his back to her but he must have sensed her presence. 'I was looking for you.'

He offered no apology for the liberty he was taking and she felt incensed, but when he turned, with his short dressing-gown open almost to the waist, she shrank from his overpowering masculinity.

'Surely you can find other ways of entertaining yourself?' she asked, trying to pull herself together. Crossing to him, she almost snatched the small silver and enamel locket from his hands. She always wore it, except in the shower.

'You're fond of it?' Without protest he let it go, his interest transferred to herself as she stood before him in her thin robe. She had packed the flimsiest one she could find, so it didn't take up much room. Now she wished she had brought something thicker or had dressed in the bathroom. But she had not expected, after the restless night Dane had spent, that he would be up this early.

'Very—attractive!' he murmured, and she knew he wasn't referring to her locket. He was gazing at her body, her long, slender legs, almost as clearly visible as if she'd had nothing on. Protectively she folded her arms over her breast. 'I've had it a long time,' she mumbled, surprised that he didn't recall giving it to her before they were married. She had seen it in a junk shop window and he had bought it for her and she had treasured it ever since. She had discovered it was quite valuable but had never considered parting with it.

Then, as something told her he did remember and she flushed, he confused her when, instead of mocking her about it, he asked instead, 'Did it surprise you, finding me here?'

'Yes,' she replied frankly.

His mouth thinned. 'I'm not trying to take up where we left off, Eden. It was your idea to come to Shetland and you don't have to stay if you don't want to.'

'I said I'd stay until next week,' she retorted, adding unhappily, 'Do you want rid of me that much?'

He smiled with a flash of white teeth, reaching out to run a hand over her abundance of fair, shining hair. 'I don't think I ever wanted rid of you that much,' he confessed huskily.

'Dane . . .?' as her eyes flew open with her mouth, her heart hammered wildly against her rib-cage. The morning was quiet and there were just the two of them. Suddenly they might have been the only two people in the world. Eden's throat clogged, not allowing the light words, which might have changed the charged atmosphere between them, to escape. She gazed into the banked fires in his grey eyes and somehow couldn't move.

'You were a lovely girl,' he muttered, his hands falling to her shoulders. 'You've grown into a beautiful woman and I can still remember what you felt like in my arms.'

He drew her into them now, his head bending to let his lips touch hers before she realised she should be drawing away. As soon as he touched her something leapt between them like a wild thing, a searing current that scorched. It left Eden feeling she was being blinded by lightning, unable to hear or see. In the hospital, when Dane had kissed her, she hadn't been in his arms. Now, as she felt the whole impact of his hard, lean body, she didn't know what was happening to her. His teeth bit into her lower lip, his tongue caressing the bruise before pushing its way into her mouth. Eden drew a sharp breath as he pursued a sensuous exploration and suddenly she was drifting away, like a leaf at the mercy of a storm. She burned and throbbed as an aching desire invaded every cell of her body and she gave up struggling for control.

She was conscious of both relief and disappointment when the noise from a car horn penetrated the swirling fog about them and she was abruptly released. 'That will be Brown,' Dane said thickly. 'I'll see what he wants.'

He seemed to be telling her to stay where she was until he got rid of Brown, but while she was still too confused by his kisses to be sure of what he appeared to be insinuating, Eden wasn't taking any chances. Dane was bored, looking for amusement, and who better to provide it than his ex-wife, who had put herself in such a position as to be entirely at his mercy.

Hurriedly she fled to the bathroom and rinsed her hot face. Just as quickly, she applied a little make-up and combed her hair. Returning to the bedroom, she pulled on a shirt and jeans and ran downstairs. The whole operation couldn't have taken more than five minutes.

She found Dane watching Brown bringing in drinks and provisions. The drinks consisted mostly of orange juice and barley water but she did see some whisky.

'Are we having a party?' she asked drily, without looking at Dane.

'Morning, Miss Eden,' Brown replied solemnly. 'Just a few things the ladies at the canteen sent to help the boss's appetite. They can't bear to be without him much longer.'

Dane grinned. 'You can tell them I should be back by Friday.'

'You're joking!' Eden's eyes were drawn to him sharply and she frowned. 'Tell him not to be so foolish, Brown.'

'I'm not that brave, Miss Eden, ma'am.'

'Call her one thing or the other,' Dane commanded irritably.

Brown looked embarrassed. 'She looks too young to be a married woman,' he mumbled inexplicitly. 'I can't decide.'

Eden felt her cheeks burn as Dane's glance rested derisively on her thick plait and blue jeans. 'I'm going for a breath of fresh air,' she announced mutinously. 'If you can't wait for breakfast you'll have to cook it yourselves!'

When she returned, without feeling much better, she found Brown in the kitchen but no sign of Dane.

'Gone back to bed,' Brown informed her before she could ask. 'Said he would wait until you were back from the beach for his breakfast. I've had mine so I decided to stay and make some for both of you. I often do for the guv'nor in the mornings, if I'm early or he's busy.'

The coffee was percolating, the bacon smelled good. Eden thanked him gratefully. She also noticed he had mopped the floor while she'd been out and that the washing machine was on. 'I don't know what we should do without you, Brown,' she confessed.

While Dane was resting, after Brown had gone, she went to the study and closed the door, then rang her mother. 'Is Jonathan all right?' she asked, as soon as she got through.

'He's having a wonderful time,' Irene enthused. 'Why not leave him with us for another week?'

'He still has a week left,' Eden replied dismissively. 'I should be back in town by the eighteenth. I'll expect him home then.'

'Have you told Dane yet?' her mother enquired quickly, as Eden said goodbye.

'No, not yet,' Eden retorted shortly. 'He's still not well enough. I'll have to wait.'

As she finished, she thought she heard a noise outside but there was no one there when she opened the door. Running upstairs she found Dane sleeping. She gazed at him closely for several seconds, to assure herself that he was, then sighed and went down to the kitchen to begin preparing lunch. She had been silly to imagine Dane had listened to her conversation with her mother. He wasn't the kind of person who eavesdropped, and, if he had, she didn't think he could have made much out of it.

He got up again after lunch and spent the rest of the afternoon in the study. Eden heard him on the 'phone continually but knew better than to interfere. She was coming to recognise him as quite a different person from the one who had remained stamped on her memory from their last quarrel. He had always been decisive and commanding but she realised she had forgotten about his sense of humour and how attractive he could be. He expected a lot from those who worked for him but, despite this, all his staff appeared to have a great respect for him. When she wasn't anxiously trying to anticipate his reactions over Jonathan, she found she could talk to him on a deeper, more satisfying level than before. If there was a slight tension between them, she supposed it wasn't surprising, considering everything, but on the whole, apart from missing Jonathan, she found herself amazingly content just to be with him.

During dinner, for which he joined her downstairs, that evening, she told him about ringing her mother earlier. 'I've been going to mention it all day,' she said, 'but you've been busy.'

He hesitated, rather warily she thought, then nodded. 'How is she?' he asked casually.

Eden glanced at him quickly and saw he wasn't really interested. 'She's having a good time.'

'Your mother always did. Is she still away?'

'Yes,' Eden didn't want to talk about it. It was too involved with Jonathan and she might give something away.

Dane, looking elegant and somehow disconcertingly sophisticated in black pants and shirt, raised a dark brow contemplatively. 'Doesn't she resent having you still on her hands? She was always ambitious for you.'

'She still is,' Eden retorted impulsively.

'I thought by now she would have had you married off to at least a lord.'

'Don't be stupid,' Eden said shortly.

'You obviously aren't keen to leave the nest again.' He glanced at her keenly over the top of the glass he raised. 'I wonder why?'

'Perhaps once bitten . . .' she shrugged, apprehensive of revealing she had left the nest, as he called it, long ago, for fear, with his rapier intellect, he began doing some shrewd thinking and happened to hit on the truth. And wasn't Bill Fraser still expounding the need to keep him calm?

'Or are you too comfortable to take another risk?' he jeered.

'Of course not,' she denied coldly.

'Four years ago,' he retorted curtly, 'when our divorce was made absolute, I nearly offered you the alimony I'd withheld. When you didn't apply for any through the lawyers, I realised your father was providing for you.'

'Dane,' she protested uneasily, 'that's all water under the bridge now. Why persist . . .?'

'Maybe I'm curious,' he stared at her keenly. 'Does it take less pride to accept help from a father than a husband?'

'You stopped being my husband.' She laid down her knife and fork and pushed her plate away.

He glanced at the food still untouched on her plate then at her pale face. 'It might be better,' he suggested softly, 'to talk of something else. I don't wish to spoil your appetite.'

Eden wasn't reluctant to take up his offer. Yet, at the same time she felt curious. Dane had no compunction over mentioning their divorce but he seemed to avoid the intervening years like a plague. She had no such reluctance herself, regarding him.

'You were always ambitious,' she murmured, serving them both with the chocolate soufflé she was so good at making and which Jonathan would consume by the gallon, if allowed. 'Did you manage to get as far as you wished?'

'Far enough,' he grunted.

She smiled faintly. 'I imagined you installed, eventually in a director's office in London or maybe New York. It was quite a surprise to find you here.'

'Success usually finishes up in an office,' he said drily. 'I know I seem to spend much of my time in one.'

'But within a stone's throw of the action?'

'If possible.'

His answers were short, unrevealing, she didn't seem to be getting very far. 'What exactly is your position with Burford Oils, Dane?' she frowned.

His eyes hardened. 'You're getting like your father, aren't you, Eden?' he jeered. 'I recall him asking the very same question, only he called me Sutherland.'

Eden flushed. What a fool she was! Would she ever forget her father's patronising tones and that Dane should believe her like him in that respect made her wince.

'Forget it,' she muttered tersely. Talking to Dane was like threading one's way through a minefield. He was bound to be prickly but she didn't feel up to inviting and bearing the brunt of his taunting remarks.

'You haven't seen anything of the islands yet,' he began talking about them abruptly, as if he was as keen to find a less controversial subject as she was.

'No,' she forced a smile, 'there hasn't been time, but what I have seen, so far, appeals to me.'

He quirked a sceptical eyebrow. 'They can be pretty grim.'

'I wouldn't argue with that,' she said slowly, 'but I've always had great faith in first impressions. My own, anyway.'

'Really?' his brow rose a fraction higher, and while she knew what he was hinting at, she ploughed on regardless.

'You must know, yourself, how some people and places appeal instantly and others don't.'

He nodded, with no mockery this time. 'I'll show you around, as soon as my head's better, and I know what you mean. For me, the Shetlands have always had an odd fascination.'

'Oil must have made a vast difference to them?'

'I would like to have known them before we arrived,' he mused, 'though I believe there were big changes before that. In the nineteen-fifties there was electricity and water to rural areas; the nineteen-sixties saw the economical revival of fishing, an expansion of the knitwear industry and a remarkable improvement in agriculture because of reseeding and such like bringing greater profitability to farms. I sometimes think they might have been better without the discovery of oil that followed. The economy might have grown more slowly but that might not have been a bad thing.'

Eden frowned. 'You can't mean you think oil is?'

'No,' he shrugged, 'I couldn't work for something I didn't believe in but you can't compare the Shetlands with, say, Texas. Oilfields bring expansion, new ports, airfields, drilling, building new rigs, but the oil boom has also brought steadily rising costs on all goods and services, which hits those not directly employed by the oil companies on high wages.'

'Benefits weighed against disadvantages?' Eden looked at him with interest. 'Do you talk much to the islanders, Dane, or are these merely your own impressions?'

The grey eyes held her gaze. 'I know a lot of them. I have, in fact, many good friends among them. I don't think you can live in a community for any length of time without becoming part of it. But oil didn't bring any great geographical changes to the islands or their climate. Both can be formidable. So,' he added curtly, 'before you decide you'd like to settle here for good, you'd be wiser to consider the harsher aspects of it.'

What made him think she was thinking of doing that? She stared at him, her eyes puzzled. 'You're way ahead of me,' she protested, 'but it was wonderful on the beach, this morning.'

'Was that the only thing about this morning that was wonderful?' he mocked.

She flushed and hoped he would never guess how hard she had tried not to think of the incident he was clearly referring to. 'I believe it's time you were going upstairs,' she glanced at the clock stiffly. 'Bill Fraser isn't going to be pleased if he comes tomorrow and finds you exhausted.'

'That'll be the day,' Dane said drily, but he let her help him to bed with surprising docility, which made her feel sure that he wasn't as fit as he pretended to be. She wasn't surprised when he fell asleep almost instantly.

It was during the night that she heard him groaning and hastily grabbed the thin robe, which was all she had available and rushed to his room to see what was wrong. He was tossing and turning, obviously having bad dreams, and she suspected the sheets, which were tangled tightly around him, weren't helping. She tried to straighten them out but he woke before she could manage it and stared at her with dazed eyes.

'You were having a nightmare,' she answered his unspoken question.

'A dream,' he amended hoarsely.

'A bad one by the way you were tossing and shouting.' She wondered if he had been reliving the accident on the rig. 'Can I get you something, if you're

over the worst of it? I was just trying to straighten your
sheets.'

'A drink, maybe? We could have a cup of tea
together?'

The way he was looking at her seemed to make him
vulnerable and much younger. It was obvious he didn't
want to be left alone, for all his light dismissal of his
bad dreams, and her heart went out to him. She felt his
aches and pains, his mental agony as her own and
longed to put her arms around him. How many times
had she wanted to do this, since coming here? She
gulped and turned away, not daring to count.

'I'll go down and make some,' she said hastily, 'if
you're sure?'

'Yes,' he sighed, with a weariness she tried not to
hear.

In the kitchen, she made the tea, setting it on a tray
with a packet of biscuits and carrying it back to the
bedroom. She had only used the landing light when she
had gone in to him earlier, but he had put the small one
on by his bedside and the glow from it was soft and
intimate. Eden couldn't see a place to put the tray as
every top seemed cluttered with Dane's papers, so she
sat on the edge of the bed and balanced it on her knees.

'This is cosy.' He grinned, stirring sugar in his tea
and taking a biscuit. He crunched his way through three
of them before Eden finished her first. His returning
vitality amazed her and she felt a twinge of envy,
forgetting how much she possessed of it herself.

'Yes, very,' she agreed, finishing her tea.

'Did we ever do this when we were married?' he
quipped. 'Or were we too busy doing other things?'

Eden let out a short sharp breath and realised she
was trembling slightly. She rose to put the tray on the
dressing-table, for fear he should notice. 'You forgot
my cup,' he called, but, when she returned for it, he put
it swiftly aside and grasped her wrist. 'Stay and keep me
company for a while,' he coaxed. 'I don't think I'll be
able to sleep again.'

'I'm sure you will.' Yet her eyes searched his face and she hesitated.

'You didn't used to be so reluctant,' he taunted gently.

She realised he was only teasing, but a tremor of desire shuddered through her at the memories he evoked. 'I don't think it would be wise,' she murmured frankly, trying to break the spell he was creating, 'to stay.'

'Do we have to be wise?' he asked huskily.

She knew what he meant. They were accountable to no one but themselves and a friendly talk might be all he had in mind. No—she sighed for such juvenile thinking. Dane was a man, issuing a very male invitation, but he wasn't forcing her. The ball was in her court. What happened next might be up to her.

She was torn both ways as he pulled on her wrist until she was sitting on the bed again, only this time much closer to him than she had been before. She tried to move away but a weak, sensual need undermined her. His gaze was like a physical thing and she was bitterly conscious of the taut, masculine strength of his body. He was using only light persuasion but her heart began beating so fast it deafened her. Her whole being seemed to be waiting, crying out, begging for her to stay.

His voice tempted with a velvet quality. 'We're both lonely.'

'Yes.' It was the merest whisper for loneliness was something she had never allowed herself to admit to since they parted. Resistance fading, she closed her eyes, sinking into the warmth of undreamed of possibilities which shut off all doubtful thought.

His hands brushed away the hair that had fallen over her cheeks then cupped her face to raise it gently. 'You're so soft,' he breathed in a thickened voice that was not quite steady. 'I thought I had forgotten.' His fingers slid through her hair, curving the back of her neck, bringing her nearer.

Like a sleepwalker, Eden swayed towards him, aware

of the slight parting of his lips as they brushed her own. She knew she should draw back but her body seemed alive and pulsating with a thousand different sensations. She moved mindlessly, instinctively reaching out in the darkness to twine her arms around his neck. As he gathered her to him, his arms closed about her under her thin robe, slipping it away until she was naked against him.

When Dane lifted his head at last, she was dazed, her soft mouth trembling and bruised by the hard urgency of his long kiss and her ears were drumming with the hungry roar of her own blood.

'I want you,' he breathed, eyes glittering beneath lowered lashes.

She wanted him but his words unexpectedly jolted her. She had been lost, rendered off balance by his seducing voice and passionate kisses. Now she realised what she was inviting by her mindless response. She was confused but not so badly that some flickers of returning apprehension didn't get through to her.

Coming briefly to her senses, she tried to push him away but his reaction was immediate and effective. She gasped as his mouth parted hers again then left a burning path down her neck to the swell of her breasts. She clutched at him blindly, holding him to her as a swift surge of desire turned the protests on her lips to sighs of pleasure.

'We'll regret this,' was all she could manage to scrape from the chaos of her mind.

'Why?' he paused a moment though his hands continued caressing her, smoothing her hair and flushed cheeks as if she was a child in need of reassurance. 'We're two adults, Eden. Once we shared something I've regretted letting go so easily.'

'You must have had other women since?' she murmured unevenly.

'How do you think I'm able to compare?' he retorted.

'Well I can't!'

To her mortification, he pounced on it immediately.

'You mean there hasn't been anyone for you, in between? What about the faithful Mr, wasn't it, Lawson?'

Miserably she shook her head.

'You didn't have to answer that,' he said thickly. 'I think I knew.'

She felt humiliated that he should think no other man had wanted her but she wasn't prepared to confess that she might have lost count of the men she'd said no to because she had wanted no one but him. Staring dazedly into his hard, sensual face, she was suddenly conscious of how true this was. Yet might not an affair with another man have been safer than the step she was in danger of taking now?

Striving desperately to get rid of the melting desire inside her, which was depleting her ability to think, she pushed her hands against Dane's chest but he refused to take any notice of her mute appeal. She gasped as he threw aside the sheets and drew her so close that the roughness of his chest and thighs scratched her bare skin, but she clung to him involuntarily as his hands slid down her body to fit her hips to his. She was powerless to speak or even breathe properly, and when his mouth found hers she met it with a passion she would never have believed herself capable of.

An unrestrained violence seemed to enter both of them then. Eden was aware of feelings more intense than anything she had known before. She felt she was dissolving into him with no will left of her own while Dane's hands and mouth grew savage with a driving urgency that seemed beyond him to control. Her breathing quickened, in tune with the hoarseness of his and she was unable to deny what her body was telling her so eloquently.

He moved over her and possessed her. His lips were moist and firm, his body hard, and as he groaned she cried out. And then they were joined and lost in an ecstasy which spiralled higher and higher until it finally consumed them completely.

Eden clung to him, burrowing her face in the warmth of his shoulder as the thud of their heartbeats slowed. She lay quietly, too stunned by surprise that anything could be more perfect than what they had already shared. They had always been compatible but never to quite this extent. Tonight, the world had rocked and shattered about them and she knew she wouldn't let him go. Trembling, beneath a wealth of new emotions, she tried to speak to him then suddenly realised, to her startled surprise, that he had fallen asleep.

CHAPTER FIVE

DISMAYED Eden eased herself away from him. Exhaustion must have overcome him and she was reminded of how ill he had been. She felt a surge of shame and remorse that she might have helped to make him worse. Cradling his head against her shoulder, she put her arms around him and curled up against him in the big bed, prepared to stay there for the rest of the night. Then suddenly she thought of Jonathan and gave a start of dismay. When she told Dane about him would he think she had deliberately tempted him to make love to her in order to soften his reaction when she told him he had a son?

And this reminded her that she wasn't married to Dane anymore. For the last hour she had been acting like a girl reconciled with a loving husband, rather than a divorced one. She had no real hold over him and he had never loved her. Nor had he ever pretended he wanted her back permanently, on any pretext whatsoever.

Despairingly, Eden returned to her own bed and lay shivering. Would she be willing to marry Dane again, if he asked her? Her cold face grew hot in the darkness as she realised how much she would like to. She loved him deeply. It had come to her while he had been showing her the heaven still to be found in his arms, and she had accepted the knowledge hazily but gratefully for it had made their reunion seem absolutely right. Now, though, she knew the future was up to Dane. If they were to remarry, he must be the one to do the proposing this time. Her hands clenched in shame as she remembered her own blind confidence at eighteen. She could never bring herself to repeat that performance again, supposing she remained single for the rest of her life!

The next morning Dane surprised her by bringing her a cup of tea to bed. 'Returning the compliment,' he said gravely, 'before I leave.'

'Leave?' she sat up, gazing at him sharply. She had slept too late but this didn't bother her nearly as much as what he was saying.

'The office,' he enlightened her briefly.

'The office!' She didn't try and hide her alarm. Brushing back the tumbled hair which she hadn't combed since his hands had tangled it in the night, she protested anxiously. 'You can't! What will Bill Fraser say?'

'I'll have a word with him,' Dane dumped the tray in her lap and glanced at her derisively. 'You won't have to make any elaborate excuses for me, he won't be coming here. Not today.'

'But you aren't well enough . . .'

'No? Whatever makes you think that?' he asked silkily.

'Oh . . .' she could have hit him for the sheer insolence in his eyes as they travelled over her. 'You may not be as fit as you think,' she said thinly.

'There's only one way of finding out,' he returned her mutinous stare blandly. 'I said I was going to work on Friday, remember?'

'Regardless?'

'Never that regardless,' he grinned. 'If I think I'm about to collapse I'll come straight home.'

'I suppose Brown will be driving you?'

'He's waiting. So's my secretary.'

'Good luck, then,' she retorted waspishly.

He paused in the doorway, turning to look at her again. 'Will you still be here when I get back?'

'It depends,' she said shortly, not having any faith at all in his supposedly lightning recovery and determined to be on the 'phone to Bill Fraser, as soon as his back was turned!

'You don't have to hurry.' He smiled but his eyes were curiously blank. 'I like your cooking, though I shan't mention it to the ladies at the canteen.'

Her cooking might be all he liked! Tears glistened in Eden's eyes as she heard him depart. Never a word regarding what had happened during the night, apart from a taunting reference to it. Was it something he just wished to forget? Perhaps that was what had driven him out this morning? He found her company embarrassing?

Assuring herself that she didn't care, Eden rushed to his room to ring Bill Fraser. Locating him at the hospital, she hurriedly explained the situation, finishing with a despairing, 'I couldn't stop him!'

Bill murmured a few soothing words then asked, more professionally. 'Have you noticed anything since yesterday to give the impression that he's not so good?'

'N-not exactly,' she replied, glad Bill couldn't see her hot cheeks.

'Then I don't think we have much to worry about,' he said cheerfully. 'I promise to keep an eye on him, Miss Petrie will too, and she knows where to find me, if need be.'

Eden sat thinking this over on Dane's bed, her fingers tapping agitatedly on the sheets which she suddenly realised were stone cold. How long had he been up? she wondered anxiously. Going downstairs, she found cold coffee in the percolator she had washed out the previous evening. He must have been up since at least six o'clock, she calculated. A hollow foreboding ate into her. She didn't know how bad his concussion had been. Doctors rarely divulged everything and Bill Fraser was no exception, though he may have told Dane a lot more than either of them had told her? But she didn't try and persuade herself that Dane's condition had not been serious and she felt sure that by returning prematurely to work, he was running a terrible risk.

When he didn't ring by eleven o'clock and there was no sign of Brown, she decided to walk into town. She didn't want Dane to think she was spying on him but she felt she must try and find out what was going on? She was discovering that being concerned for him was

very much a part of the new kind of love she felt for
him. When she had been married to him, she couldn't
remember ever feeling as anxious about him as she was
now. Even though she had known his job was
hazardous and that he operated in dangerous parts of
the world, it had never bothered her unduly that
something might happen to him. She had been more
concerned for her own position as a neglected wife, but
now it was only Dane she could think of.

She might have enjoyed the walk if she hadn't been
so worried over him. The road was long and lonely but
the morning was so bright and fresh it was a pleasure to
be out. The various scents of the islands, mingling with
the salty tang of the sea, was bracing. Eden was so busy
admiring the views that she didn't notice the mist and
heavy clouds creeping over the horizon. By the time she
did, she was halfway between the house and town and
regretted not bringing a coat with her when a torrential
shower came down, soaking her.

After the rain a cool wind blew up and other showers
followed. She was sniffing unhappily long before she
reached the town, and wishing she had never come out.
The streets were as wet as she was and she decided
against having another look around. All she wanted to
do was to find Dane and see how he was, then beg him
to let Brown take her home again.

Spotting a light raincoat in a shop window, she went
in and bought it, along with a matching hat, hoping,
when she put them on that it might disguise how wet
she was so Dane wouldn't be cross. She had no idea
where his offices were and asked the girl in the shop if
she knew where she could find them?

Following the directions she was given, she found
them easily and went nervously inside. They were large,
there seemed to be dozens of people scurrying about, all
too busy to spare the rather uncomfortable looking girl
in a plastic mac, more than a cursory glance.

At the enquiries desk, when she was told no one got
to see Mr Sutherland without an appointment, she

gazed at the clerk in dismay. Fortunately Miss Petrie, at
that moment escorting an important personage to his
car, noticed Eden as she returned and whisked her
straight up to her office.

'Now, my dear,' she said briskly, after inviting Eden
to sit down. 'I can't pretend I'm not surprised to see
you on such a terrible day but I presume you're looking
for your husband?'

Eden nodded unhappily. 'I've been so worried about
him, I couldn't stay away.' She swallowed, adding, as
Miss Petrie's eyes frowned on the ill-fitting waterproof,
'I bought this in a shop along the street. I left London
in such a hurry, I hadn't time to bring much.'

'So I understand.' The stern-faced lady acknowledged
drily. 'It's a pity you aren't able to visit your husband
more often, Mrs Sutherland, then you could leave some
clothes here suitable for our island weather.'

Eden glanced at her warily wishing, as she had been
doing for days, that she had made her position clear
from the start. As she hadn't, it seemed she must
pretend to be Dane's wife until she left and be prepared
to put up with being accused of neglect. Not that Miss
Petrie was actually accusing her of anything but she
would have had to be blind not to have seen the silent
rebuke in her eyes and totally without imagination not
to have known what she was hinting at.

'I don't think Dane should have come back to work
so soon,' she said quickly, rather than mention, that
unless Dane asked her, she might not be here again.

'It was a very important board meeting,' Miss Petrie
explained.

'But not as important as his health, surely?'

Miss Petrie shrugged. 'You must have realised long
ago that your husband has a mind of his own. I did
suggest a postponement but he wouldn't hear of it. It's
over now, though, so if you like, I'll tell him you're
here?'

A moment after Miss Petrie buzzed him, with a speed
that startled Eden, he was in the room, towering over

her angrily. 'If this is your idea of a joke,' he snapped, 'I don't appreciate it.'

She looked away from his furious eyes. 'I only came to see if you were all right,' she muttered tightly. 'That can't be a crime?'

'You walked?' he exploded. 'In the rain.'

'It was nice when I started out,' she sneezed.

'That's all we need!' he explained, as if she already had pneumonia. 'How long have you been sitting around in those wet things?'

'I've just arrived,' she sneezed again, 'well, practically.'

'Come into my office,' he rasped, 'I'm nearly through.'

Eden followed him meekly, feeling like a dog at his master's heel. 'I don't want to be a nuisance,' she protested. 'If I could just borrow Brown to take me home . . .'

'I'll take you, myself, in a few minutes.' He shut the office door behind them with subdued force. 'How wet did you say you were?'

'I didn't . . .'

'Eden!' He was pale but whatever it was he had been doing this morning, didn't appear to have depleted his vitality. Turning, he whipped off her hat then dropped it to run his hand over her wet hair. 'That blow I received must have affected my vision, you seem extremely wet to me.'

'I had my mac.' She tried to push him away.

'Since when?' He didn't budge. 'I suspect from the smell of it, it's brand new. How long have you had it— ten minutes?' As though seeking further proof, he undid several buttons and stood staring, tight-lipped, at the way her soaked blouse was clinging to her taut breasts.

Aware that further prevarication was useless, she nodded miserably, hating the way her pulse was racing as his eyes roved over her.

'You're still totally lacking in sense!' he grated, letting go of the front of her mackintosh as if it had suddenly stung him.

'You haven't that much, yourself,' she retorted rashly. 'You've been to a board meeting.'

'It concerned the blow out on the rig,' he said shortly. 'It was imperative that I should attend. I could have held it at the house but it could have been embarrassing for you as some of those who came were from London.'

'I'm sure I wouldn't have known anyone, though the man with Miss Petrie,' she frowned, 'seemed vaguely familiar.'

'Exactly,' Dane snapped. 'He was on his way to the airport and, if you'd met, he might have recognised you.'

Which might have been just as embarrassing for Dane? she thought dully. 'Is a blow out very serious?' she asked, to change the subject.

'Any accident on an oil rig has to be treated seriously,' he replied curtly. 'But the danger can usually be minimised if a few basic procedures are adhered to and not ignored. However, let's not waste time discussing it. I have a few calls to make and I want to get you home as soon as possible.'

Eden was surprised that it was after three when they arrived home. It must have been later than she'd thought when she had reached Dane's office. He'd had a working lunch but offered to make something for Eden while she showered.

'I'm nearly dry,' she objected. 'I don't need a shower.'

'Do as you're told,' he dismissed, making for the kitchen.

If he hadn't spoken so sharply, she might have obeyed but she disliked being treated like a mindless idiot. She went to the bathroom but merely flung her damp jeans and shirt in the bath, after taking them off, and rinsed her face and hands in warm water. She was shivering, but not that badly.

Dane must have sensed she was ignoring his instructions for suddenly the bathroom door was flung open and he strode in. He seemed not to notice she was wearing only her bra and panties, both little more than scraps of lace. 'You have five seconds to get under that shower,' he rasped. 'Otherwise I'll put you there myself.'

She could see he wasn't joking, which only added to the outrage she felt at such an intrusion. She was trying to remember they were divorced but, after last night, it wasn't easy, and he wasn't helping by coming in here. 'When you get out!' she snapped.

He gave her a contemptuous glance as he obliged. 'No more than five minutes,' he warned, over his shoulder. 'Your lunch is ready.'

She wasn't hungry. Peeling off her flimsy underthings, she obeyed him this time but deliberately stayed under the shower far longer than he stipulated. 'Let him rave!' she muttered to herself, with a hint of returning rebellion. It might make him think twice before ordering her about again!

The water beat down on her head and shoulders and then Dane was back, wrenching open the shower door, turning off the water. Before she could do a thing to protect herself, he was throwing a towel around her, lifting her out, taking no notice of her protesting gasps.

Despite such ruthlessness, Eden expected he would at least leave her to dry herself. Instead he stayed, his hands moving over her briskly, a look of determination on his face. In a humiliatingly short space of time, Eden found she had stopped fighting and was longing for him to throw the towel away and stroke her bare flesh. Water dripped from her hair and he removed the excess, watching her harshly as she tried unsuccessfully to keep every muscle in her body rigid until he was through tormenting her.

She couldn't think of another word that might as adequately describe what he was doing to her. Perhaps he didn't realise it but the movements of his hands was stimulating such a storm of desire inside her that there was no way she could contain it. Her legs went weak, while her lungs were so depleted of air she couldn't breathe normally. At last, making another effort, she begged, 'For God's sake, Dane, let me go.'

He looked as if it was what he would have liked to have done, but was as trapped as she was by emotions beyond his control. And her pleading, instead of persuading him to release her, appeared to have the opposite effect. Dropping the towel, he put his arms around her, crushing her to him, so tightly that she gasped. She heard him breathing hoarsely, stroking her bare back, dragging his fingers through her silky hair with a violence that brought both pleasure and pain.

His eyes glittered feverishly as he bent his dark head towards her, his lips silencing her before she could find the breath to speak again. The first bruising impact of his mouth hurt as he assaulted hers with almost savage demand. It was as if he was angry with her for what she was doing to him and he forced her lips apart with a tempestuous hunger she couldn't fight. She made a futile effort to evade him but he only laughed harshly against her mouth. Then suddenly she was responding to his violence with a reckless, insatiable need of her own. The feelings tearing through her became too wild to be satisfied by merely being close to him and she clung to him dizzily, meeting the savage demand of his arms and lips with a passionate abandonment.

There was something frantic in their devouring attempts to meet the vibrant, compelling desire surging between them. Their bodies strained closer while hands grasped with urgent impatience. Eden thought Dane became part of her long before he took total possession of her. She never knew when he discarded his clothing. A dangerous heedlessness closed her mind to everything but the ruthlessness of his lovemaking. A heated weakness swept through her and she was lost in a dark whirlpool of sensation.

He made love to her right there in the bathroom, on the carpet which wasn't thick enough to disguise the hardness of the floor, but she might have been floating on the softest bed for all the difference it made. If anything it seemed to accentuate the primitive forces rioting within her as she met the savage thrust of his hard male body. Every movement he made, every sensuous exploration of his hands and mouth, made her writhe with exquisite sensation until fierce ripples of release began flooding her, and, as they reached the peak of ultimate fulfilment together, he forced her beyond the edge of control into a vortex of ecstasy which at last brought release from his own needs.

Afterwards, he rose abruptly to his feet and walked into the shower without a word. He might have glanced at her but he didn't speak. Again there was the silence she was coming to dread.

Dizzily she picked herself up, wrapping the discarded towel clumsily around herself as she almost ran to her room where she flopped helplessly on to the bed. She wanted to gibe and shout at him but what would be the use? She might have fought a lot of things but the wall of silence he erected between them couldn't have been more effective, had it been ten feet high and a thousand feet wide!

Suddenly Eden felt terribly weary, to the point of exhaustion. Relaxed, with her skin sensitive from the shower, she hadn't been able to fight him. Not that she tried to deceive herself it would be easy to fight the amazing new magic that consumed them each time they made love. It even seemed to exist in every glance they exchanged. And she was sure Dane was aware of it, too, for hadn't she experienced the strength of his response, the violent, climactic shudders that had torn through his powerful body, yet he shunned talking about it as if it was a plague. Probably—a chill hand touched her heart—because he wanted nothing more from her than this.

She sighed, lying back on her pillows, trying desperately not to believe it. If only they had still been married, how wonderful it might have been. Why hadn't they decided on a separation? Plenty of people opted for this instead of divorce, then got back together again with the minimum of fuss. Realising how much she loved Dane now, made the difference that hurt. She longed to do things, like running her hands over his face, tenderly soothing and kissing the lines of strain from it, things that didn't necessarily have to do with sex. That was good, too, she blushed in the dimness of the overcast light, but not everything. She wanted to tell him a thousand times a day that she loved him, and she had a strange yearning to perform small, wifely tasks such as picking up his clothes and putting them away, but she couldn't, not with the invisible barrier of their divorce between them. And soon there would be something else for she had no excuse to put off telling him about Jonathan any longer and she could almost guess what his reactions to that would be.

The weekend passed slowly yet in some ways too quickly. When sometimes she found Dane looking at her thoughtfully, a moment or two seemed to appear like hours as she waited in vain for him to say something about the future. He never mentioned making love to her, either, and though she admitted it could have been embarrassing, she couldn't believe it would have been worse than having to endure his apparent determination to pretend it had never happened. But on Sunday, when he showed her something of the island, the day seemed to go on wings.

Brown drove them as Dane said he didn't feel up to it, but when she expressed concern and told him she didn't mind staying at home, he retorted that he was feeling tired, not ill.

'You can't leave without having a better look around,' he said firmly. 'So far, you've seen nothing.'

'I don't want to be a nuisance.'

He grinned at her. 'Once you were a nuisance all the time but didn't seem aware of it. Now you aren't but you keep on insisting you are.'

She flushed. 'I didn't realise I was as bad as that!'

He laughed. 'There were things I liked about you.'

They were travelling towards the south of the island and not wishing Brown to hear such a conversation, she changed it adroitly. 'I always believed Orkney and Shetland were more or less the same but I gather they are really different.'

Dane nodded. 'They are so often spoken of in the same breath that it's commonly believed they are the same, but in fact they are both very different. Both are a group of islands with the Atlantic on one side and the North Sea on the other and both were discovered by Norse seamen and came under the jurisdiction of a Norse ruler, but, in other respects, I think there is contrast rather than resemblance.'

'I won't have time to discover the differences myself,' Eden remarked wistfully, 'I can see that this island is very beautiful.'

'More so than Orkney, which has better soil,' Dane replied. 'It is dangerous to generalise but I've studied the islands in the years I've been coming here,' he smiled, 'An oil man's always interested in the geographical aspect, you know, and I've come to the conclusion that the Orkneymen are farmers who happen to be born close to the sea, while the Shetlanders have been seafarers who took to the sea for their livelihood and regarded their islands as convenient harbours. The Orkneyman is devoted to his farm and animals while the Shetlander spends more of his time fishing.'

'And the people, themselves?' Eden asked.

'Again, just my personal opinion,' Dane said, glancing at her with a new warmth, as if he approved of her interest. 'Nowhere is there any dislike or suspicion of strangers but I've found the Shetlander easier to talk to and he usually has more to say than the Orkneyman. The people of the Orkneys I'd say are shier but they're extremely hard working and, once you get to know them, make every good friends.'

'Thanks for explaining,' Eden said tentatively as he paused, then felt foolish when he observed sardonically.

'You can't explain people, communities, centuries of their life in a few short sentences. I've just tried to give you the general picture. You'd have to do years of studying and research to understand completely and even then you might still have a lot to learn.'

Feeling quietly rebuked, Eden smiled ruefully. 'I'll begin reading it up straight away. That's something I can do in London.

'Sure,' he agreed curtly, then leaned over to speak to Brown.

They travelled to the south of the island first where he showed her the Sumburgh Airport, which had been entirely reconstructed since the oil companies had arrived. Next they went up the west coast, past Sandwick and Scalloway, both large bases for offshore servicing, if not so extensive as those at Lerwick. Then they continued on to Sullom Voe, where the major oil-related developments were centred in one massive complex. It was here, Dane told her, where he usually did most of his work and spent much of his time.

Since 1975, he explained, as Eden gazed about her in astonishment, Sullom Voe had been transformed with the building of tanker jetties, large oil storage tanks, enormous power stations and acres of workshops and other facilities, and, as Europe's biggest oil terminal, had the capacity to handle millions of tons of crude oil a year. Thousands of men and women were employed on the site, all of whom had to be housed, fed and entertained in an area where previously only sheep had roamed the heather covered hills.

Once she had recovered from her first startled surprise at the sheer size and complexity of everything, there were so many questions Eden wished to ask that she didn't know where to start. Dane, however, seemed to think she had seen and learned enough for one day and whipped her off to visit a croft at North Nesting, on their way home.

An elderly couple farmed the croft and they were invited into their house for a cup of tea. Brown stayed in the car so Eden and Dane went in alone. Dane had explained that the couple were friends of his and when

he introduced Eden, though they shook hands with her
courteously, she sensed rather than saw their disapproval. Then she realised that, like a lot of others,
they thought she was Dane's wife and neglecting him. It
wasn't until she accepted a large slice of newly baked
soda bread with her tea and praised the delicious home
made strawberry jam that they thawed sufficiently to
relax with her and offered to show her around the
house and land.

'I like your friends, Dane,' she said wistfully as they
returned home. 'They seem so—well,' she searched for
the word that was evading her, 'content together.'

'They've been together a long time, over fifty years,'
Dane replied, 'And that's how it should be.'

'They must be some of the lucky ones,' she retorted,
more bitterly than she realised.

'Perhaps they worked at it harder,' he retorted drily.
'People around here don't give up easily.'

'You mean like we—I did?'

'It's too long ago, Eden,' he muttered curtly. 'You
can't go putting the past right after six years. It's better
to cut your losses and forget, than worry yourself to
death wondering where you went wrong.'

There might be worse advice to follow, she decided as
she prepared dinner that evening, but while a few weeks
ago she might have whole-heartedly agreed, she knew
that for her it was going to be one of the most difficult
things she'd ever had to do. If Dane didn't ask her to
marry him again, which didn't seem likely, she guessed
all the signposts she could see pointed to heartache.

She would have told Dane about Jonathan after
dinner but he was called to the 'phone. He was still at it
at ten o'clock and looked so tired that she felt she must
wait until the next day. Longer than that, she refused to
allow herself to consider.

With this resolve stiffening her mind, she rose early on
the Monday morning and made his breakfast. It was
probably for the last time. After today, he might not wish
to know her. Waiting until Brown tooted, she deliberately

followed him to the door and asked if he would spare her an hour that evening as she had something very important she wished to talk to him about.

'That sounds rather ominous.' He frowned, pausing halfway to the car, watching the sun catching her fair hair and turning it to gold. 'You aren't thinking of leaving?'

'Yes,' she admitted reluctantly, 'but it's not that, though I'd appreciate it if you'd get Miss Petrie to arrange a flight for me, tomorrow. I'd do it myself but I don't know the necessary procedures.'

'Why the hurry?' he snapped.

'You might understand,' she whispered, 'after this evening.'

It wasn't an easy day. She spent it tidying the house and washing everything she could lay hands on. She regretted not having brought many clothes as the packing of a few heavy suitcases might have tired her enough to stop her thinking of Dane. She couldn't forget how tall and attractive he had looked as he wished her a rather curt farewell, that morning. After preparing dinner, she went for a last walk along the shore to try and relax but found it impossible. Dane was going to hate her after tonight and she found this difficult to come to terms with.

He was gone twelve hours but came home earlier than he sometimes did. 'I've arranged your flight,' he informed her. 'You won't have to break your journey, this time. You'll go straight to London.'

A sense of fatality settled on Eden. 'Thank you,' she murmured, unable to add anything else for the tears in her throat.

Dane appeared to enjoy his dinner though he refused a second helping of anything. She wondered anxiously if he would be all right on his own?

Earlier, when she had spoken to Bill Fraser on the 'phone, he had assured her Dane would be. 'As long as you don't stay away so long, this time,' he had teased. 'He needs you.'

Everyone, apart from Dane, seemed to think he needed her. He might need someone but she was the wrong woman. She couldn't tell Bill Fraser this though. Instead she'd wished him a rather tense goodbye and said nothing.

'Shall we take our coffee to the lounge?' Dane interrupted her thoughts to make the suggestion after they had finished eating. 'There's something you wish to discuss, I believe?'

'Yes,' she muttered, rushing to switch off the percolator which had been bubbling away for at least five minutes.

He watched, seemingly idly, while she filled two cups and placed them on a tray. Casually he picked the tray up and followed her from the kitchen. 'I've waited a long time to hear why you came. I began to think it was for my sake but I've a funny feeling that I'm in for a rude awakening.'

Eden glanced at him sharply, startled that his intuitive reasoning should contain more than an element of truth. 'It was partly for your sake,' she replied unevenly, 'but there is something else.'

He waited for her to sit down before he sat down himself. 'If it's just about money, why spoil our last evening over something so trivial? Anything of that nature can be settled through our solicitors. For looking after me so well, I'm prepared to be generous.'

Colour flooded Eden's cheeks as she guessed what he was hinting at but she refused to be side tracked, even by disparagement! 'It's not trivial,' she retorted.

'So,' his brows quirked mockingly as he rose to pour them each a brandy. 'What's the big secret? You're beginning to intrigue me.'

She ignored both the brandy and her coffee. 'You're going to be shocked.'

It wasn't a good start. His grey eyes sharpened though he observed casually enough, 'I'm not easily.'

She tried again. 'I have to go back to when we parted.'

He gave her a puzzled look. 'I thought we'd decided to forget all that?'

'I wish we could,' she answered without thinking, her face paling.

'What's stopping you?'

She had never had much time for cowards but had to force herself to stop hesitating. 'After we parted, Dane,' she repeated, her voice suddenly strained, 'I discovered I was pregnant. That's why I can't forget.'

He seemed to reel, as if she had struck him. 'My God!' he breathed, his face ashen. 'Why didn't you tell me? I had the right to know, hadn't I?'

She closed her eyes and opened them again, reluctant to meet the swift anger in his. 'I realised afterwards you had. At the time, I was so furious and upset that I didn't feel you had any rights.'

Dane opened his mouth to speak and closed it again. He looked suddenly older and as if he was having difficulty in putting something into words. 'I—you had a termination? Is this what you're finding so difficult to tell me?' He stared at her grimly, 'I suppose it was your conscience that brought you rushing up here.'

'Dane—I . . .'

His tongue lashed her. 'Wouldn't it have been better if you'd kept your sordid little secret to yourself? What good did you imagine it would do, telling me now? Do you hate me so much that you deliberately tried to finish me off? When you came to the hospital, how frustrated you must have felt when your nerve failed you.'

'Dane!' she pleaded almost wildly, 'Will you listen . . .'

Once more he cut her off. 'I accept you were very young but it was my child as well as yours.'

Her eyes flashed with the brief anger that enabled her to say sharply. 'I didn't have a termination!'

It was obvious he was taken aback. His eyes were suddenly not grey but black and full of an incredulous fury which seemed to scorch her. 'Wait a minute, let's get this straight,' he exclaimed. 'If you didn't have a termination, does this mean I have a . . .'

'Son,' she finished the sentence that seemed to be sticking in his throat, with little less difficulty. She felt like weeping. She had thought she might feel angry or apprehensive when she told him, but never like weeping! 'He was born nearly six years ago.'

Dane stared at her, his face still white, then he sank his head in his hands and groaned. When he raised it again both his eyes and voice were like chips of ice. 'I can't believe it! All this time and you have never said anything, never even given me a hint of anything, or let me near him. What sort of a woman are you, Eden, that you could do that to a man?'

CHAPTER SIX

EDEN felt a sick sensation in her stomach at the hate in his voice. 'I tried to tell you. I wrote when I was in hospital.'

'Hospital?' he jerked upright.

'Having him. I wrote but you never answered.'

'You did?'

'Two letters,' she assured him.

'I never received anything.'

'I sent them through Burford Oils.'

'You can't have done. I would have got them,' he said curtly.

Eden recalled she had given them to Trevor to post. He had promised to post them and she had checked later. But had he? Or had he lied? Or was it Dane who was doing that? Staring into his pale, furious face, she knew it was Trevor she should be doubting. After all, she had only told Dane she was ill. With some justification, if he had received her letters, he could have said he would have come if she had explained about the baby. No, it must have been Trevor, possibly with the approval of her mother. He must have destroyed them.

Dane appeared as stunned as she felt. 'You told me, when you wrote, about the baby?'

Her thick lashes flickered uncertainly. 'Not exactly. I said I was ill.'

'Why not the truth?'

She couldn't blame him for asking the same question she had asked herself. She had realised he might come because of the baby but she had wanted him to come for her sake. She had desperately sought for some assurance that he still cared for her and if he had come for any other reason, she had feared she might never know.

'I thought it would seem like blackmail.'

'I can't understand you, Eden.' Angrily his eyes bored into her. 'Were you so full of vanity that you had to prove I would run if you lifted your little finger? A man's son, next to his wife, is usually the most important thing in his life, yet you had no qualms, after one feeble attempt, about keeping all knowledge of him from me.'

Eden gazed at him numbly. Did she deserve such severe castigation? She tried to justify herself a little. 'How could I know you hadn't received my letters? I thought, when you didn't come, that you didn't want anything more to do with me. You never tried to get in touch, yourself.'

His icy eyes reflected he wasn't buying that! 'So far as I was concerned, I had no reason to. You left me in no doubt of your opinion of me, the last time we met. It was you who demanded a divorce and swore you never wished to see me again.'

She winced and asked bitterly, 'Don't you ever regret things you say in anger?'

'If I do, I make sure that the other party knows.'

'But you went away. I had no idea where you were.' Her eyes darkened with remembered pain. 'I thought you had finished with me.'

'You seem to have done an awful lot of thinking along the wrong lines,' he said contemptuously. Getting up he paced the room then returned to her, his hands clenched. 'So you had my son, almost six years ago, and decided to tell me about him only when you believed I was about to depart this life and wouldn't be able to claim him. Why?'

'I don't know why!' She looked at him distractedly, 'That's not an easy question to answer, Dane, but I don't think it was for any one reason.'

Bending suddenly, he grasped her arms, lifting her out of her chair. 'Do you expect me to be satisfied with that?'

His savage face was within inches of her own and she trembled. She wasn't being deliberately evasive but there were things she couldn't divulge without sinking her pride. She hadn't realised, until she came here, how much she loved him but she might have guessed why she'd consistently rejected all other men. Subconsciously she suspected, it was her love for Dane that had driven her here and she had used Jonathan as an excuse. She might not have forgiven herself if Dane had died without knowing about Jonathan but she was sure that it was her overwhelming love for him which had brought her so urgently to his bedside.

'You'll have to be satisfied.' She drew a choked breath, 'I'm sorry I didn't make more effort to tell you about Jonathan before this. I'm beginning to understand how you must feel . . .'

'Is that his name?'

'Yes. I remembered you saying it was your father's name.'

'Rather a mouthful, Jonathan Sutherland,' was the only comment he made. 'Who does he look like?'

'He's dark—grey eyes.' She hesitated nervously, 'I think he's like you but you'd have to judge for yourself.'

'I intend to.'

Which he made sound so ominous that she gazed at him in dismay. He was still holding her and she could feel her whole body responding to him. That it could, when she was otherwise so tense, startled her. She could feel her breasts grow taut, a familiar warmth invading her limbs. Being close to him, when they'd been married, had always affected her but never intolerably, like this. Despite everything, she was having to use all the willpower she possessed not to throw herself into his arms. There was so much explosive chemistry between them that she didn't know how to fight it. It was what had been missing in the other men she had dated. She might have settled for an affectionate relationship with Trevor without realising what she was missing. Yet Dane was making it very clear that he despised her, so she could only look forward to an empty future.

'Dane?' she whispered, her mouth dry. 'What are you going to do?'

'I'm certainly not leaving him to be brought up by your parents.'

She frowned as she looked up at him. 'They aren't bringing him up. I'm doing that myself.'

'I don't believe it.'

She had to convince him. 'I haven't lived with them since Jonathan was born,' she said proudly. 'I found a job and a room.'

Dane's surprise was evident, his scepticism, even more so. 'You never mentioned this before.'

'Because you might have wanted to know more and you hadn't to be upset.'

'Was this why you waited so long to tell me? Why you offered to stay and look after me?'

'Partly, I suppose.'

They stood staring at each other, Dane coldly, Eden with misery in her eyes. There was no softening of his harsh expression, as far as she could see.

'I'm upset now, if that's the word you like to use for it,' he said grimly. 'So what's the difference? All that warm response, the living sensation you were in my arms, what was it all about? An effort to soften my eventual wrath when you told me about Jonathan?'

This was so exactly what she had feared he would believe that she shivered. 'You think that was all it was?'

'From what I can recall,' he drawled, 'you would do anything to get your own way and avoid criticism.'

Her eyes widened. 'I've changed, Dane. Don't you realise. Sex . . .'

She had been about to say sex didn't come into it when he interrupted rudely. 'As far as that goes, we ignite instantly, but then we always did.'

Why was she driven to pursue it, when there were so many other, more crucial matters to discuss. Colour creeping to her pale cheeks, she murmured, 'Never quite like this.'

'You maybe had practise.'

'There's been no one,' she murmured involuntarily.

'I might have believed you,' he grated, 'if you hadn't been so good at deceiving me.' His grey eyes glittered cynically. 'I can find women like you anywhere but I have only one son.'

He might have hit her! Eden's hopes didn't fade—they died so swiftly there'd be no hope of reviving them. 'I have looked after him,' she said dully. 'He hasn't been neglected.'

'Poor kid,' his mouth thinned. 'It can't have been much fun being in the middle of a tug-of-war between filthy rich grandparents and a young mother living perversely like a beatnik.'

How much more could she stand? Eden went cold as he continued to stare at her scornfully. 'It hasn't been like that, Dane. I have a shop.'

'Shop?' Suspicion coloured his terse query. 'What kind of a shop?'

'Antiques.' She was as short as he was.

He threw back his head and laughed. It had a harsh sound. 'You wouldn't know the first thing about them.'

'I do!' she looked at him resentfully. 'My father's elder brother was a curator of a museum. I spent a lot of time with my aunt. Their house was full of the loveliest old things and Aunt Adela took me with her to places like Christies and Sothebys, almost before I could walk. They taught me a lot I never forgot, even if I could never afford their kind of things.'

'But they started you off?'

Didn't he believe she was capable of doing anything on her own? 'No. They've been dead a long time and my cousin in the States got everything they had, including their money. I found a job in an antique shop and eventually took it over with the help of a small legacy left to me by my grandfather. I don't make a fortune but it's enough.'

Dane asked coldly. 'And what do you do with my son while you're busy playing shop? Push him under the counter?'

She could stand his derision. She supposed it was only to be expected, but she resented that he didn't take her work seriously. 'He goes to school, and there's a Mrs Willis in the flat below mine who looks after him when necessary.'

'Why did you stop living with your parents?' he asked abruptly.

She didn't mention how the scornful remarks in his last letter had eventually broken the fetters that had tied her to them, enabling her to make a life of her own. She glanced at him warily. 'I thought the time had come to be independent.'

'Yet you allow your parents to take my son to France or wherever, whenever they like?'

She wished he would stop referring to Jonathan as his son. Cold fear suddenly clutched at her heart as she stared at him. Surely he didn't intend taking Jonathan away from her?

'It's only for two weeks.' She looked at him, mute appeal in her grey eyes. 'They're his grandparents. I don't let them spoil him but I don't feel I have the right to deprive them of his company altogether.'

'You had no compunction about depriving me.'

'I've explained,' Eden replied tautly. 'I didn't think you wanted anything to do with us. For all I knew, you could have married again.'

'Were you hoping I had?' his eyes narrowed. 'Even if I had, I would still have had rights regarding Jonathan, you know.'

He believed in rubbing it in. Her lips moved stiffly. 'Well, you know about him now and, while I don't expect to be forgiven, I don't want him to suffer.'

'Where am I supposed to be?' Dane asked derisively, and, when she glanced at him questioningly, explained tersely, 'His father.'

'Oh, I see,' she flushed. 'I told him the truth, that we're divorced. There was nothing to hide and he's very intelligent.'

'You just hid my existence.'

'I told him you worked for an oil company and a few other things,' she retorted, glad now that she had though it hadn't been easy. Every time Jonathan asked questions about his father, answering them was like opening up a wound.

Dane didn't look impressed. 'I won't ask what the other things were.'

Eden frowned and jerked away from him to sit down again. Suddenly her legs felt too weak to support her any longer and she couldn't bear the strange mixture of contempt and desire in his eyes. 'What are you going to do, Dane?' she implored.

'Are you hoping I'm going to say, nothing?' His anger reached out to her, making a mockery of the distance she had tried to put between them. 'There's plenty I intend doing. To start with, I'm following you to London just as soon as it can be arranged.'

'To—meet Jonathan?'

'What else?'

She seemed to be making a mess of things. 'I only meant, you won't just barge in . . .'

'Do you take me for a fool?'

He wasn't making it easy. She met his dark glance helplessly. If her mind hadn't been so befuddled, she might have found it easier to be more explicit. 'He could get a terrible shock. I'm not sure how children react to this kind of thing?'

'Sensitive, like you, is he?'

His sarcasm hurt but she forced herself to go on. 'What do you know about children, Dane?'

His mouth curled. 'I've been denied six years, when I might have gained some experience.'

She was wasting her time trying to talk to him. Maybe he's suffering from shock? she thought, but dismissed such a suggestion immediately. Men like Dane Sutherland were too tough to be shocked by anything. The hardness of his eyes and mouth were confirmation of this, if she was looking for any.

'This conversation doesn't seem to be getting us

anywhere,' she muttered wearily.

'As far as I'm concerned,' he said tightly, 'everything is settled. I come to London and meet my son, then we share him. If I'm not satisfied he is being brought up properly, I'll apply for custody. And don't imagine you wouldn't have a fight on your hands, Eden. I'm a lot better off now than I used to be.'

Eden worried about this desperately, during the next few days. She had no idea of Dane's exact financial standing but she didn't doubt that he was much better off than he used to be. It was the aura of power that she didn't like. He had always had it but never to such a pronounced degree and she shuddered to think of it being used against her if they didn't agree over Jonathan. His threats, she knew, were not to be taken lightly and, because of them, she scarcely slept for the first few nights after returning to London.

She rang her mother as soon as she returned, to ask about Jonathan, but was informed by the housekeeper, who always travelled with them, that her parents were away cruising with friends and Jonathan was with them.

Eden felt like exploding but managed to ask calmly. 'When are you expecting them back, Nora!'

'Maybe tomorrow or the next day, Miss Eden.'

'When they do come back, would you ask my mother to give me a ring before she does anything else?' Eden requested.

This information seemed to add to the worries she already had. What right had her mother to take Jonathan on a boat trip? He never sat still and could easily get into mischief! If Dane heard he might say it was dangerous. She was sure her mother wouldn't do anything deliberately to endanger Jonathan's life but she was inclined to be careless while her father wasn't as young as he used to be. Jonathan should have been home now, anyway, instead of sailing around the Mediterranean!

Of Trevor she heard nothing. This puzzled her

slightly until a mutual acquaintance mentioned that he was abroad on business. This must be why there had been no frantic 'phone calls to the Shetlands? She seldom told Trevor where she was going but he usually had devious ways of finding out. It was ironical though, that when she especially wished to see him, he wasn't there.

Dane rang to see if she had got safely home. He had seen her off himself at the airport. Careless of the interested eyes of the ground crews, he had put his arms around her and kissed her passionately. 'Don't struggle,' he had muttered against her lips. 'You wish to give the impression that we are a devoted married couple, don't you?' Without saying anything more, or allowing Eden to, he had kissed her again then released her gently to go and have a word with the pilot. She had boarded the plane, a brisk wind blowing her long hair about her face, and it had been a long time before she was able to stop herself trembling.

He rang every night. They were not particularly friendly calls, neither did he betray any animosity. After the third night, Eden guessed that he was really checking to ensure she was still here and hadn't ran off somewhere, taking Jonathan with her.

When she heard from her mother, she asked her to bring Jonathan home immediately. 'And I mean it!' she said.

'It's not convenient,' Irene protested.

'Briggs can bring him,' Eden retorted. 'He will enjoy the trip.'

'Is there any particular reason for such haste?' Irene snapped.

'Dane is coming to London and wants to meet him,' Eden replied.

Irene's gasp of horror came clearly over the line. 'I told you, you should never have gone to Shetland!' she wailed. 'Never say I didn't warn you!'

'Dane happens to be Jonathan's father, Mother. He has a right to see him.'

Irene sniffed. 'Is he demanding his rights? That is what's important.'

'Mother! So far he hasn't demanded anything!' Her mother must wait and see, the same as she was having to do. 'Just get Jonathan back to me, as soon as possible.'

Jonathan arrived the next afternoon with Briggs who was returning to France again but said her parents might be home by the weekend. After her conversation with her mother, Eden wasn't surprised. When Dane rang to say he would be in London the following evening, she knew she must do her best to prepare Jonathan for his visit.

She waited until he was having his breakfast, so he would have all day to get used to the idea but wouldn't spend the night worrying. He was having cornflakes, orange juice and an egg. She made plenty of toast and there was honey and thick marmalade but she wasn't hungry.

Topping up her coffee, from which she had only taken a couple of sips, she cleared her throat and said awkwardly. 'There's someone coming to see you today, Jonathan.'

'Who, Mum?'

He was listening to his cornflakes crackling after he poured the milk on and barely glanced up when she said, 'Your father, as a matter of fact.'

'Is he nice, Mum?'

She looked at the top of his curly head, his face was buried in his cornflake bowl. 'You'll have to decide that for yourself, but I think so.'

Jonathan looked at her then, his eyes bright. 'Has the oil ran out?'

She shook her head, feeling too tense to smile. 'That isn't the reason he's coming.'

'Is he going to live with us?'

She hesitated, thinking he had inherited Dane's directness. 'He works in the Shetlands, Jonathan. These are islands off the North East coast of Scotland, a long way from London. Somehow, I don't think he will be able to live with us.'

'Do you want him to, Mum?'

Did Jonathan realise what kind of questions he was asking, she wondered? The rate his cornflakes were disappearing didn't suggest that the news of his father's eminent arrival was disturbing him unduly. 'I don't know,' she replied honestly, for although she loved Dane and wanted him, she wasn't sure how they would get on living together again. She didn't want to give Jonathan a more definite answer—she wasn't even sure that she could, for fear he repeated it to Dane.

'Are you going to the shop today, Mum?'

Eden stared at him. She supposed at his age it was difficult to sustain interest in someone you'd never met, even a father. 'I expect so,' she sighed. 'We can't live on fresh air.'

'Then can I play with Peter?' he asked with a wheedling smile. 'He's got some smashing toys his auntie brought him back from holiday.'

Peter was the boy next door. 'I'd better take you around before I go and check it's all right with his mother, then I'll see Mrs Willis so she'll know where to find you for lunch.'

On her way to the shop, she had a word with Jennifer Graham who was a widow with a young son, like herself, but whose husband had left her well enough off to be able to live without having to take an outside job. She was always happy to let the two boys play together while Eden, as Jennifer led quite a busy social life, could usually return the favour by looking after Peter when she wished to go out of an evening.

Eden had rather a hectic day at the shop and not a very encouraging one. A chest she had paid a good price for turned out to be a fake and a small ornament, worth all of fifty pounds, disappeared when she wasn't looking. She closed at six and was glad to, even if she wasn't exactly looking forward to the evening.

Every time she thought of Dane coming, she broke

into a cold sweat. She loved him and found herself
worrying for fear Jonathan didn't like him. She
imagined Jonathan staring at his father with dislike in
his eyes and wondered how she would be able to bear it
if he did? Strangely she didn't feel jealous of sharing
Jonathan with Dane. It was because she couldn't be
sure what the outcome of their meeting would be that
she was uneasy.

Mrs Willis had started dinner for her, all she had to
do was dish it up. By seven-thirty the chicken should be
done to a turn and the vegetables already looked
succulent. Despite the anxieties of the day, Eden began
feeling hungry. She hoped Dane wouldn't be late. She
had made up the bed in the spare room earlier that
morning. Dane hadn't said if he wished to stay but she
hadn't wanted to be running around searching for
sheets at the last moment.

Jonathan seemed to have forgotten about him, he
was watching the TV when the doorbell rang. It was
seven o'clock. Eden had just managed to shower and
dress and set the table.

'Dane——' She knew she sounded breathless as she
opened the door but her heart was hammering so hard
she was thankful she could speak at all. She was pleased
to see he was wearing a pair of black cotton pants and a
sweat shirt beneath a casual jacket. He looked big but
not nearly so formidable as he looked in his business
suits. Jonathan might like him better.

His grey eyes angled over her trim figure before
returning to her face, and her legs felt as if they'd give
way any moment. Then his glance went to her mouth
and she saw a muscle move in his jaw. 'I've arrived,' he
said tautly.

They stared at each other for several more long
seconds before Eden managed to find her tongue to ask
him to come in. He followed her into the small hall
where he shed the kind of rucksack holdall he had slung
over his shoulder. He seemed relaxed though she
noticed he was pale beneath his tan.

'Have you completely recovered yet?' she asked impulsively, believing this might be the cause of it.

'Sure,' he shrugged. 'Only a few tender places.'

He glanced around curiously and she wondered if he was trying to decide if it was a good enough place for his son to live? 'Where is he?' he asked suddenly, jerking her out of the confused state she was in.

'Come this way,' she sounded like an usherette at a cinema but she couldn't help it. She opened the lounge door, revealing Jonathan with his back to them, watching television.

He turned his head only slightly as Dane and she went in. 'It's a good programme, Mum.'

It was a Walt Disney film. Eden heaved a sigh of relief. It could have been anything—she hadn't checked. Jonathan didn't usually stay up this late. She only allowed it on special occasions.

For one awful moment she thought Jonathan was going to ignore Dane then suddenly he seemed to realise there was a tall man standing beside his mother. 'Hi!' he said eagerly, scrambling to his feet. 'Are you my father?'

'I am,' said Dane gravely, moving forward, holding out his hand. 'Hi, Jonathan.'

Jonathan placed his small hand in his – he seemed to like the adult status it implied. He looked up, craning his neck. 'You're awfully high.'

Dane smiled. 'You might be yourself, one day.'

Jonathan nodded. 'If I take after you.' He turned back to his beloved telly. 'Do you like Walt Disney?'

'One of my favourites,' Dane nodded, availing himself of the place Jonathan made beside him on the couch as Eden sat in a chair.

Jonathan's eyes were glued to the screen but Eden could see he was curious about his father. After a moment he said. 'I've been allowed to stay up specially to meet you. Will you still be here in the morning?'

Dane glanced at Eden. 'That depends on your mother.'

Eden refused to read things in that question that probably weren't there. 'I made up the bed in the spare room,' she said quickly. 'I don't know what your plans are but you're welcome to stay if you wish.'

Dane looked at her coolly. 'I expect to be in London for at least two or three weeks and I'd rather stay here than in a hotel.'

'Are you on holiday?' Jonathan asked.

'No, not exactly,' Dane answered. 'I can please myself whether I work or not, but,' he glanced from his son to Eden enigmatically, 'I think I have better things to do.'

After they had had dinner and Jonathan had gone to bed, Eden made a fresh pot of coffee and told Dane to help himself to drinks. He declined a drink but accepted some more coffee. It was slightly stuffy in the lounge for it was a hot August night, but Eden knew if she opened the window the noise of passing traffic might be deafening. She couldn't wait to ask what he thought of Jonathan but was aware of being oddly hesitant. Dane's face wore a closed expression, as though his thoughts were private.

At last, as if aware of her restraint and taking pity on her, he said quietly. 'He's a bright boy. You've done well.'

Such praise went to her head, bringing unexpected tears to her eyes. 'I'm sorry you missed his first years but there's a lot more to come.'

When he nodded but made no attempt to discuss the future, she felt a stab of disappointment which she hid with a forced smile. If Dane had no intention of sharing the future with her, she must learn to accept this. All she could do, meanwhile, was hope.

'How long has he been going to school?'

She started, having been miles away, dreading and dreaming. 'A year. He got a place before he was five. He isn't six until Christmas.'

'He was a Christmas baby?'

'Boxing day.' Would she ever forget the terrible loneliness? Her mother had been there but she had cried

so much for Dane, thinking how wonderful it might
have been had he been there . . .

Then Dane wanted to know where Jonathan went to
school and she found herself explaining all kinds of
things, such as what she considered his faults and
virtues, his likes and dislikes, what he liked doing most.
She suddenly realised she'd had no one to really talk to
about him, not in quite this way, until now.

'He plays a lot with the boy next door,' she told him
about Jennifer. 'But he often prefers to play by himself
in his bedroom and he reads a lot. He's a very good
reader, at least I think he is, for his age.'

Dane listened attentively, his eyes never leaving her
face, and when she paused self-consciously and
apologised for going on, he merely seemed disappointed
that she had stopped. 'I suppose you could leave me a
few things to discover for myself,' he smiled.

'I didn't mean to hand you a ready formed opinion of
him,' she flushed.

'I know you didn't.' His smile became gentler, 'I
appreciate you've given me the basics, and you're the
only one who could have done that, but we'll probably
never see him quite the same way.' He grinned. 'My
mother could never see my faults for all my father never
stopped pointing them out to her.'

Eden glanced at him anxiously. 'I'm fairly strict with
him but he's not used to a heavy hand.'

'Don't worry. I had too much of that in my own
youth to inflict the same kind of punishment on any
child of mine.'

Eden felt so relieved that she was prepared to say
generously. 'I think he likes you.'

'He accepts me,' Dane shrugged, 'because he hasn't
had time to really digest me. Tomorrow he will
probably get down to calling me Dad and weighing me
up properly. And even then, young as he is, he might
have reservations. At the moment, I possibly represent
an unknown quantity, rather than a change in his life?'

Eden lowered her eyes warily. Was this meant as a

warning? Dane didn't appear angry, this evening, as he had been in the Shetlands, but she'd be a fool to assume it wasn't still there underneath.

'How much influence do your parents have?' she heard him asking abruptly.

'I told you—none.' When his eyes glittered derisively, she exclaimed impatiently. 'Why won't you believe me, Dane? Jonathan and I usually go for lunch on Sundays but, otherwise, we seldom see them. Anyway, I think Jonathan's too young to worry them unduly yet. If they've any influence to exert, it's usually directed at me.'

He looked at her sharply, seeming suddenly to have lost interest in his son. 'In what way?'

'Oh,' she tried to shrug casually, not wishing to mention Trevor, 'they haven't approved of me for years. The work I do, the way I live. You might see for yourself.'

'I intend to.' He got up, pulling her up beside him. Slipping a hand around her shoulders, he bent to kiss her softly on the lips. 'That's for preparing the ground for me with Jonathan. It can't have been easy.'

She had to tease, to hide a longing to throw her arms around him. 'You consider that ample reward?'

He smiled ruefully but as lightly as she did. 'It will have to do for tonight. I guess I'm not as Herculean as I thought I was. Or I've been doing too much, trying to get down here in a hurry.'

She looked at him, feeling a surge of compassion. 'Why don't you have a bath and go to bed?'

'I don't think I'll refuse.' He kissed her gently again then released her, leaving her feeling desolate and curiously empty.

Lying in her own bed that night, Eden wished he was there beside her. The bed was big enough, being king-size. She had got it cheap, in a sale, when she first came here and hadn't been able to afford to furnish the spare room. She had never had anyone to stay but she'd thought it might be useful if she had. She wondered if she hadn't had Dane in mind, all along, rather than a casual visitor?

She could see that Dane was going to get on well with Jonathan. She knew Jonathan. If he didn't take to people from the start he never did. He had never taken to Trevor. Not that he was ever rude to anyone, he was too well-mannered, but he never got close to them. She would go as far as to say that the obvious liking he showed for Dane had little to do with Dane being his father. There had just been an immediate affinity between them, such as there had been between Dane and herself, in Cairo. All those years ago, she could still remember how good he had been with her, humouring her like a child, with the same understanding he was showing Jonathan until, in her case, more intense feelings had taken over.

She got up at seven and tidied the lounge and did a few more things to help Mrs Willis before she started getting breakfast. She was going to ask Dane if he would like breakfast in bed when she heard him in the shower. Going into the kitchen, she began squeezing fresh orange juice then putting sausages under the grill and cutting the rind off the bacon. Ten minutes later, when Dane and Jonathan appeared together, everything was ready and she smiled at them warmly. Dane looked rested, as if he had enjoyed a better night's sleep than she had, and he was wearing a pair of jeans and an open-necked shirt that didn't suggest he was going to the office. She glanced at the way his jeans hugged his muscular thighs and swallowed.

Both Dane and Jonathan ate a good breakfast, then Jonathan asked. 'Shall I play with Peter this morning, Mum, or do I stay with Dad?'

'I think you and Peter could both come with me,' Dane suggested, his eyes on Eden. 'We will drop your mum off at her shop first though, unless she would like to take the day off and come with us?'

'We can't live on fresh air,' Jonathan quoted brightly.

'Jonathan!'

'That's what you always tell Trevor.'

Eden hustled him out while Dane rang for a taxi and followed.

'So Lawson is still around?' he drawled in her ear.

'I see him occasionally.' She didn't want to say more with Jonathan around but she was dismayed at the harder expression in Dane's eyes. He clearly believed her short answer was intended to remind him she was free to see who she liked.

She felt no happier, either, at the look of interest on Jennifer's face when Eden introduced them. She only said he was Jonathan's father but Jennifer knew she was divorced.

No sooner had they collected Peter than the taxi was there, speeding them to the shop. London looked dry and dusty, that morning, and the paint on the shop, almost as shabby as that on her flat. She hoped Dane wouldn't notice.

He offered to take her out for lunch but she said she would be too busy. 'I'll just get a sandwich, you can pick me up later. That is, if you have nothing better to do?' she added somewhat stiffly, still rather shocked at the way he had smiled at Jennifer. Eden wondered if she reminded him of that dark-eyed nurse? They had the same kind of eyes.

CHAPTER SEVEN

DANE said he would call at the shop early to take her home but at five, when there was no sign of him, she rang the flat.

She received the impression that he had forgotten about her. 'Sorry,' he apologised, when she asked what was keeping him. 'I was talking to Jennifer. She came to collect Peter.'

'Where's Mrs Willis?' Eden asked sharply.

'Busy in the kitchen.'

While you're busy in the lounge, ran her suspicious thoughts which she didn't voice. This didn't stop her from grinding her teeth.

'I'll be home later,' she said, pride prompting her to add, 'I'd as soon walk as I've plenty of time and Mrs Willis usually starts dinner.'

'Just as you like,' he agreed coolly. 'But I'm taking you out for dinner.'

'It's too late for Jonathan,' she protested.

'Mrs Willis is going to look after him,' Dane said smoothly and rang off.

Eden felt so annoyed by such high-handedness that she lingered deliberately at the shop longer than she normally did, but she walked the mile between it and the flat so quickly that she probably made up the lost time. Try as she might, she couldn't stop thinking of Dane and Jennifer. It wasn't that she was put out about Dane talking to the other girl but it did remind her sharply that she had no hold over him. He might be staying at the flat but they weren't living together. She wasn't even sure that he wanted her anymore. Last night he had pleaded tiredness but when had that ever stopped him! Ordinarily she might have been ashamed of such thoughts but lately she had been so confused that she seemed to have lost all control over what she was thinking. One thing was certain. It was no use pretending she and Dane were still married, or even going to be.

He was playing a game of draughts with Jonathan when she got home. The television was off and there was no sign of either Jennifer or Mrs Willis. The scent of Jennifer's favourite perfume hung on the air and Eden took a disparaging sniff of it. She didn't know why but wished she hadn't when Dane's eyes glinted knowingly and he asked innocently if something was wrong?

'Dad made my supper, Mum,' Jonathan jumped two of Dane's men when he thought he wasn't looking but put them back when Dane told him firmly to stop cheating. Eden could tell he was impressed rather than disgruntled by his father's astuteness.

'I hope he made you the right things?' She knew she sounded pettish but suddenly she resented Dane looking so relaxed while she was sure she must look like a hag after working all day.

'Scrambled eggs, jelly left over from lunch, a big glass of milk,' Jonathan recited. 'Dad's a great cook, Mum.'

'I'm sure he is,' she muttered.

Dane eyed the faint hostility in her face with interest but merely smiled.

Eden flushed and asked quickly. 'What's all this about taking me out to dinner, or have you changed your mind?'

'No, why should I?' He rose to take the cardigan she was still holding and laid it over a chair. 'All you have to do is get ready, I'll do the same. Everything's arranged. I booked a table for eight-thirty. Wear something nice.'

Jonathan was stacking the draught's away obligingly. 'This is really a kid's game, Mum,' he was saying. 'Dad's going to get me something different tomorrow. One of those games you play on TV. He's got a chess computer but it might be too old for me.'

She would see about that! Eden's lips firmed.

Although it might not be such a bad idea. She wouldn't mind having a go at something like that herself but she would have to be careful. Dane appeared to be an expert at everything and she didn't want to be shown up in front of Jonathan. Dane already looked like becoming a big enough influence in his life.

Jonathan put the draughts neatly in their cupboard then turned eagerly to his mother again. 'Did you see Dad's car at the door? It can pass most things.'

She had noticed the tough looking sports car outside but hadn't connected it with Dane. People in the area were apt to park wherever they could find a space, and she had known strange cars to be in the street for days. 'Where did you get it from?' she asked shortly.

'Company,' he murmured, watching her idly. 'Now, are you going to get changed? We'll never make it if you hang about much longer, unless we share the bathroom.'

Shooting him a frowning glance, she told Jonathan sharply it was time he was in bed.

'S'all right, Mum,' he reached up to give her a quick hug as she bent to kiss him good night. 'I promised Mrs Willis I'd be in bed when she came back. I 'spect I'll be asleep.'

Eden, having a contrary desire to be awkward, lingered in the bathroom far longer than she usually did, but the thought of spending the evening dining and perhaps dancing with Dane soon had the blood dancing eagerly through her veins. Speeding to her room, she found a white, summery dress with billowing sleeves and a full skirt of material so light it seemed to float. In it she looked blonde and very beautiful, the only colour about her being the soft pink of her mouth and nails and the slight, becoming flush on her cheeks.

Suddenly she wondered what Dane would be wearing? Always before, when he had told her to wear something nice, they had been going somewhere out of the ordinary, but surely he wasn't contemplating taking her to a top-class restaurant in jeans?

She flushed for her doubts when he emerged from his room, resplendent in dark jacket and tie. 'You didn't bring that with you either,' she remarked, referring, this time, to his clothing. 'Have you hired it?'

'No.' His eyes glinted, 'Not that there'd be anything wrong with that but this happens to be my own. I'm surprised you don't recognise it? After we parted and I gave up the flat, I left a few things at the office which come in handy during my odd visits home. I collected this when I went for the car.'

She knew he had given up the flat. After Jonathan was born she had visited it several times until she had realised there were new tenants. She nodded, blinking back sudden tears. 'It still looks good on you.'

'You're looking good yourself.'

'Is that the best you can do?' She tried to retort lightly, ignoring the way her heart was beating as his eyes darkened over her slender figure.

He grinned, falling in with her mood. 'I believed I wasn't doing too badly, considering how little practise I get.'

'Was that what you were doing talking to Jennifer?'

'Jennifer is very nice,' he allowed, 'but so are a lot of women I meet.'

'Including your dark-eyed nurse?' she asked pertly.

His brows rose mockingly. 'I'm really spoiled for choice, aren't I?'

Eden was saved from having to answer that by having to go and let Mrs Willis in. Mrs Willis was inclined to chat until Dane said firmly they should be leaving.

His car was outside and, as he helped her into it, Eden asked what make it was?

'Aston Martin but far from new,' he replied briefly.

'It's very comfortable,' she said, as he shot off. Her father's cars were too dignified for her taste, while Trevor's were always so brand new and flashy that she was scared Jonathan would leave sticky marks on them. She wondered how long Dane had had it? 'We don't really know much about each other now, do we Dane?'

'I'd like to know more about you,' he replied, which made her realise she might have mistaken his attitude regarding the shop, this morning. He hadn't apparently been as indifferent as he'd appeared to be, but if he thought he was going to do a full-scale investigation into her affairs, then he would have to think again!

Somehow, she felt the evening had got off to a bad start but it wasn't difficult to forget her antagonism over dinner in a restaurant which might have been designed to soothe even the most ruffled feelings. Dane, she wasn't sure whether deliberately or by inclination, kept the conversation light and his quiet tones completed the therapy of such harmonious surroundings. When they danced together, later, she relaxed against him, her mind stirring only dreamily to wonder how everything could seem so much like old times, yet so incredibly new?

She felt as familiar with Dane as though she had known him all her life, but, as his encircling arm brought her tightly against his body, she knew that never before had she experienced the waves of high sensitivity that flashed between them now, when they were close.

It had started in Shetland, when they had first seen each other again. It was as if all that had gone before had merely been a foundation for other feelings of far greater intensity. In her saner moments she was getting to be frightened of such powerful emotions for she was doubtful that Dane was thinking of doing anything permanent about them, other than kissing her goodbye.

Dismissing such a possibility from her mind, she pressed her head against his shoulder, her fingers hovering a fraction away from his black hair. His arms surrounded her, taking her closer into his embrace and her body clamoured greedily for more. She felt the strength of his strong limbs moving against her and her heart thudded. Her lips moved and she caught her lower one in dismay, between her teeth. She had been on the verge of whispering how much she loved him! Trembling she drew back. He probably didn't know what he was doing to her but she had to get away from him before he found out.

'Would you mind if we sat down again, Dane?' she breathed. 'I feel rather shaky. I've probably been trying to do too much in the heat.'

'It has been hot,' he agreed, glancing at her pale face with concern as he immediately released her and began steering her off the floor. 'Look, why don't you take the day off tomorrow? Leave your assistant to manage.'

'I don't have an assistant,' she retorted, then flushed as they reached their table and sat down. Such a confession might not make him admire her more. 'So far I haven't been able to afford one but I can usually cope.'

He frowned but didn't press the issue. 'This business about Jonathan hasn't helped, has it? It's been a bigger strain than you anticipated.'

Was that merely an astute comment or a sympathetic one? Eden didn't think it was the latter though she might have welcomed it. 'I'll admit to feeling anxious about you and Jonathan,' she confessed. 'How long do you think . . .?'

'Eden!' Dane cut in grimly. 'I've met my son and we've a lot of catching up to do but it's not going to be done in five minutes.'

'It's just that everything seems so unsettled,' she faltered.

His eyes went even harder. 'One of the penalties you must be prepared to pay, I'm afraid.'

The muscles of Eden's throat tightened. How could she have thought, even for a moment, that Dane was sympathetic. He didn't have to face the possibility that haunted her continually, of Jonathan being taken away from her, that she might be left alone to face an empty future.

They stared at each other and she could feel the tension mounting between them again. She made an effort to disperse it. 'It's getting late, Dane. Mrs Willis will be wondering where we've got to. I think we'd better go.'

'I'll see she's well compensated,' he said.

'It's not that,' Eden told him ruefully. 'I think she's fond of her bed.'

Dane grinned. 'It must be more comfortable than the one you gave me.'

Eden felt stricken as the waiter he had signalled arrived and he settled the bill. In his car, she said, uncertainly. 'It's too small, of course.'

'Yes.' He leaned over to fasten her forgotten seat belt, a flicker of humour in his eyes. 'There's nothing actually wrong with the bed otherwise.'

Eden glanced at him then away again quickly as her eyes collided with his and she was unable to sustain his penetrating gaze. 'If I'd thought you'd be staying more than one night, I'd have let you have mine. Only . . .'

As she hesitated, he touched her hot cheek understandingly. 'That would have meant moving your things or coming in and out to get what you wanted while I was there.'

'Something like that.'

He laughed gently and bent over in the darkness afforded by the parking area to kiss her averted cheek. 'Don't worry about it, Eden,' he said softly. 'We'll work something out. It never pays to try and take all your fences in one go.'

She turned with a quick retort and never knew how it happened that somehow, as she opened her mouth it came in direct contact with his. For the next few moments she was at the mercy of a delving tongue as the tenderness evident in his former kiss turned swiftly to something else.

His arms went around her, with a tightness suggesting passion barely held in control. As liquid fire scorched through her, she leaned weakly against him, a small moan escaping her as his fingers curved her breasts. Soon her body was pulsing and throbbing in urgent response, her heart thudding in time with the pounding of his.

Then, abruptly, as a hazy part of her mind was wondering if it was possible to make love in a car, he eased from her, a dull flush on his hard cheekbones.

'We'd better go before the attendant starts snooping around,' he sighed.

Eden nodded but failed in her attempt to make light conversation on the way back to the flat. She couldn't concentrate and kept breaking off in the middle of sentences as she became totally absorbed in wondering if he meant to kiss her again, once they were home?

But in the flat, much to her consternation, he reverted to the aloofness he had shown her so many times in Shetland. After saying goodnight to Mrs Willis and slipping something into her hand, he retired to his room without even looking at Eden. Eden locked up behind Mrs Willis then sat in the lounge until she heard him in the bathroom. Waiting until she heard him come out, she slipped quietly to the hall. Her face was burning but she had to ask what was wrong?

'Dane . . .?' she began.

He interrupted with the ruthless air of a man determined she should be left with few illusions. 'My head is aching badly, Eden.'

'H-have you taken anything for it?'

'No,' he said grimly, eyes cold. 'All I need is peace and quiet.'

He was really saying he had no wish to take up where they'd left off in the car-park. The colour in Eden's cheeks deepened even further as she hoped stiltedly that he would be able to sleep. She didn't mention, as she blindly watched him retreat to his room again and firmly close the door, that she had been going to offer him her bed. Not only that, she had been going to hint she would be willing to share it.

She was up early next morning but he wasn't long in following. He found her in the kitchen preparing breakfast. The bacon and sausages were already sizzling under the grill while the fat was hot for the eggs. She was determined to show him she hadn't been fooled by his apparent collapse, the evening before, by cooking his usual breakfast. It might have satisfied the resentment inside her more to have given him tea and dry toast, but at least this let him know she had got the message! Without speaking she dumped the cereal packet in front of him as he sat down and resisted an impulse to pour the orange juice down his neck.

He was acting like he'd never dealt a merciless blow to her pride. 'Another beautiful morning, by the looks of it,' he murmured with an innocent smile.

'Depends which way you look at it,' she shot him a malevolent glance.

He drained his juice and against her will, she found herself staring at him. Did he have to look so damned attractive? She glared at him sullenly.

'I want to take you to work, this morning,' he was saying. 'I'd like to see your shop.'

'Whenever you find it convenient,' she agreed sarcastically, putting the percolator and a jug of milk on the table.

'You're spoiling me,' he murmured, 'I don't know how I'm going to manage on my own again.'

'I'm sure you'll never be reduced to that,' she snapped, meaningly, on her way to fetch Jonathan.

Jonathan was obviously tired from yesterday's excitement. 'Why do I have to get up?' he complained. 'Dad's not taking me shopping until later.'

'Because he's coming to the shop with me and I didn't think you'd want to be left here with only Mrs Willis.'

'What about Peter?'

'You know Peter and his mother always go to his grandparents on Fridays for the weekend.'

'Umm,' he yawned. 'I forgot.'

'You don't see him every day, anyway. Now hurry!' she glanced at her watch. 'I'm going to be late as it is.'

She wasn't late because Jonathan co-operated and Dane got him his breakfast while she brushed her teeth and fixed her hair then consulted with Mrs Willis about lunch. Dane might offer to take Jonathan out for it but she didn't want to come to rely on him.

Dane, very familiar with London streets and traffic, had them at the shop in no time. He parked outside and helped her in with the few things she was carrying, Jonathan on the other side of him. The showroom wasn't huge but it was quite well stocked. Eden tried to see it through Dane's eyes. He was glancing around with interest but she couldn't tell what he was thinking?

'Do you do your own buying?' he picked up an Oriental vase, one of a pair, studying it thoughtfully.

'If there's a sale locally, I do.' She began taking covers off a few things and giving other things a light dusting. 'Sometimes people bring things to me to sell, when they need money. I try to give them a fair price and leave a margin for profit, but the last owner of the business had someone who did the buying for her and I still use him.'

'Him?'

Did Dane sound jealous or suspicious? Again, his masklike face, frustratingly revealed nothing. She got on with her dusting. 'Leo Farndale's a retired army officer. He and his wife use their enthusiasm for auctions to make a little extra cash to boost their pension. I give him so much commission on every sale I make and we're both happy.'

'I thought you were the expert?'

She didn't like the sarcastic note in his voice. 'I'm expert enough to make sure I'm not landed with a lot of junk and Leo knows it. It's the only way an arrangement like this could work. The Farndales know what I like and rarely make a mistake.'

'Wouldn't it be better if you did all your own buying, though?' he persisted.

She shrugged. 'I'd have to provide my own transport. A van would be too expensive to buy, licence, insure, and keep in good order. And, while going to the auctions myself, might be more fun, it can be very time consuming. One day, when Leo gives up, I might. I'd have to think about it.'

Dane frowned as he digested this, his eyes fixed on Eden closely. In a matching cotton skirt and blouse, she looked young and charming if a little strained. 'Where has Jonathan gone?' he asked abruptly.

'Upstairs,' Eden pointed towards a narrow, rather crooked staircase. 'That's one of his favourite places. It's where I keep things I'm busy mending and polishing, including one or two old toys which he likes to play with.'

'I'll go and see what he's up to.' Dane said, but as if his mind wasn't completely on his son.

Eden watched him disappear up the staircase, her own face almost as preoccupied. Then she dragged her thoughts away from a pair of broad shoulders and decided to make coffee. There were rarely any customers before ten and at this time of the year they were mostly foreign tourists. She did have a loyal following among local people, though, who had come to rely on her for usually being able to find exactly what they wanted.

She was just about to enter the back premises, which she used as a storeroom and office, to put the kettle on when the shop door opened with a resounding tinkle and Trevor walked in. She turned, her eyes widening in dismay. She had wanted to see him badly, but not here, like this!

'Who's stolen my parking space?' he complained, before even saying hello. 'I've had to park on those yellow lines over the street and I might get pinched.'

'How often have you been here, Trevor?' she asked drily, with no compunction for his sagging face. 'I think the last time it was snowing, for you complained that the road wasn't cleared.'

'Oh, all right!' he muttered nastily. 'Point taken, but how often I come here isn't what I came to discuss,' his voice hardened belligerently, 'I want to know what's going on?'

'What's—going on?' she repeated coldly.

His mouth tightened with impatience at her haughtily

raised brows. 'Oh, for heaven's sake, come off it, Eden. You can't pretend not to know what I'm on about? You and your ex! I've just been to the flat and that old bag who looks after it said,' he mimicked, ' "Mister Sutherland is staying here!" '

Eden hid her anger at the way he referred to Mrs Willis but she didn't back down, as Trevor obviously expected her to. 'What if he is?' she asked sharply.

Trevor looked incredulous enough to drop. 'My God, Eden! Considering how he left you and never came near you, when you were practically at death's door in hospital . . .'

'Wait a minute!' Eden broke in, suddenly furious. 'I wasn't at death's door, and whose fault was it that Dane never came near me, or at least never got the chance to decide whether to or not?'

'I don't know what you're talking about.' Trevor blustered, 'But that's not the point.'

'Oh, but I think it is!' she countered sharply. 'You were supposed to post two letters I wrote to Dane.'

'I did!'

Eden had to bite her tongue to stop herself from calling him outright, a liar. 'To think I gave them to you, asked you to come so I could, because I believed I couldn't trust my mother to post them.'

He went pale but continued to bluster, though he didn't go on denying his obvious guilt. 'It was for your own good, Eden, ask your mother! Your doctors said you weren't to be upset. I couldn't take the responsibility.'

'You could have let them decide, if Dane had come to see me.'

'Damn it all, Eden, how was I to know?' Trevor muttered sullenly. 'I thought it was just some peculiar notion you'd got into your head, because of your condition? Remember you went right off tea and coffee when you were pregnant and would only drink cocoa. And if you'd really cared for Sutherland, would you have been in such a hurry to divorce him, in the first place?'

'That's enough, Trevor!' Eden blazed, 'Whatever your opinion of either my marriage or Dane, you had no right to betray a trust. I don't think I want to see you again.'

'You're angry, darling,' Trevor coaxed. 'After you calm down you would regret throwing me out, considering all there's been between us.'

'I'm calm now, Trevor. And you know as well as I do, there's never been anything between us.'

'Whose fault is that?' Trevor muttered morosely.

'And there never will be,' Eden continued, as though he had never spoken. 'Especially not now. I don't ever want to see you again.'

'You'll regret this!' His eyes smouldered vindictively, 'Just wait until your mother gets back.'

'Trevor, will you please go!'

'Oh, all right!' he retorted angrily. 'I can see I'm trying to reason with a brick wall, and I can wait until you come to your senses and realise Sutherland's a swine!'

The door slammed so hard the chimes nearly went mad. Eden stood where she was for a minute, trying to stop herself trembling, then sighed and remembered she had been on her way to make coffee. She was just plugging in the kettle when Dane spoke behind her.

'You had a visitor.'

She swung around sharply, dawning apprehension in her eyes. Trevor and she had been so busy shouting at each other that everything else had gone out of her head. It seemed incredible that she had forgotten Dane and Jonathan were upstairs. Dane couldn't have helped being aware of the quarrel going on below him.

'Jonathan?' she whispered in dismay.

'Don't worry,' he said shortly, with immediate understanding. 'I kept him sufficiently occupied, so he missed most of what you and Lawson were on about. I missed some of it, myself, but I got the gist of it.'

Eden stared at him unhappily. 'I forgot you were there.'

'Most things I didn't regret hearing,' he replied cynically, 'But I didn't particularly like being called a swine.'

'He was angry,' she faltered.

'Not as angry as I'm going to be when I catch up with him, and I hope you aren't flying to his defence.'

More like trying to avert a catastrophe, Eden shivered, recalling rumours she had heard, years ago, of the hardness of Dane's fist. 'I'm not defending him,' she denied tensely. 'I just don't think he's worth fighting over.'

'Leave that to me,' Dane advised curtly, then, more abruptly, after looking at her for a few more moments. 'I think I owe you an apology for not believing you about those letters.'

Her eyes flickered away from his guarded ones. Did his apology really mean anything? It didn't seem as if it might. 'When I told you about them, in Shetland, you didn't believe me. What happens the next time something comes up and I can't supply proof?'

When he didn't reply, she glanced at him quickly again. He looked so remote that she couldn't decide whether he hadn't heard her or was being deliberately evasive?

Then he startled her by suddenly grasping her by both arms above the elbows and leaning so close that she could see the peculiar whiteness around his mouth. His eyes bored into her, as he exclaimed, 'He talked of you being at death's door. What the hell did he mean?'

Why did she have the feeling that this question was something torn out of him, something he had tried to ignore but failed? Eden shook her head to get rid of a feeling of bewilderment. 'He was exaggerating to try and—well, justify his actions, I suppose? There were one or two complications but nothing serious.' She didn't mention that her nerves had been the cause of most of them. She had worried over Dane, missing him until she made herself ill. How Dane would gloat if he knew this.

'You've been well since?' he asked huskily.

She nodded, replying drily. 'If you need any proof, you have only to consider how I've worked ever since Jonathan was born and brought him up.'

'Convincing yourself a husband wasn't necessary, after all?'

Just what did he mean by that? 'I've not had much time to think about it,' she lied, wishing, just for once, she could read some expression in his eyes. Given the least bit of encouragement, she might have asked if he would have visited her in hospital, if he had received her letters? The question tortured her throat, having to hold it back but she was so terrified of a negative reply.

The kettle boiled, breaking the tension surrounding them as she jerked from his arms to switch it off. She reached for her jar of Nescafé and a mug, scarcely realising what she was doing.

'Don't I get any?'

His voice was back to match his eyes. Grabbing another mug, she warned over her shoulder. 'It's only instant.'

He looked amused. 'What's wrong with that? I've drank gallons of the stuff in places where you'd never find a socket for a percolator. I'd go as far as to say it's almost saved my life on occasion, and I like it as well as the other.'

'Did you return to those kind of places—after we, that is . . .?' Somehow her voice played up and she was gazing at him helplessly when, fortunately, Jonathan ran in.

'I thought you were coming back, Dad?'

Dane ruffled the boy's hair with teasing fingers as Jonathan flung himself at him. 'Your mother had the kettle on and I was tempted to stay with her.'

'For coffee?' Jonathan's eyes darkened with disgust. 'Who wants that when there's lemonade?' he looked around hopefully.

Eden sighed resignedly. 'There's some in the fridge. You can bring me the milk, while you're there.'

He skipped over to the tiny fridge, stuffed in a corner of the over-crowded room. 'One's enough,' she called firmly, as he removed two cans.

He put one back reluctantly, his mouth sulky. Eden realised he reacted quite differently when Dane rebuked him. Ignoring her, he returned to Dane. 'I'd like to see an oil rig, Dad. I think I'm going to work on one when I'm grown up. Could I come with you to Shetland?'

Dane smiled at him. 'It might depend on your mother.'

'I don't go back to school for a few weeks.'

'We'll think about it.'

Eden took a scalding drink of coffee as the shop door tinkled. Seeing the almost defeated expression on her face, Dane swallowed and said curtly. 'Finish your drink, Eden. I'll go and see what this one wants? If I need any help, I'll give you a shout.'

Eden didn't argue. Mysteriously, for the past five minutes, she had been fighting a desire to weep. She needed a moment to pull herself together.

Jonathan stayed with her. As if unconsciously sensing her distress, he gave her a warm hug then began glancing through an old comic that someone had brought in yesterday, wrapped around a plate they wished to sell. Eden tried to keep her mind on him, rather than on Dane and the rather disturbing events of the morning. He could do with some new clothes. His jeans were getting thin at the knees, his last years T-shirts were too tight. She wasn't looking forward to going shopping with him. Like his father, he had a mind of his own and if she let him have his own way he would choose clothes quite unsuitable for him. She sighed for such problems as always seems to be with her, yet couldn't find much consolation in the thought that she might no longer have to shoulder them alone.

Dane returned to reach for his coffee. 'I think she just wanted to browse.' His mouth curved with dry amusement, 'Actually, she seemed more interested in me.'

'Did she want to buy you?' Jonathan asked solemnly.

Dane laughed cynically. 'I'd be no bargain, son.'

Did she detect a flicker of uncertainty? Eden stared at him but couldn't be sure. He had too much confidence ever to underrate himself. As for being vulnerable, he probably didn't know what the word meant!

'Are we staying here all morning?' Jonathan asked next. 'We could go to the zoo, Dad, while Mum is busy?'

'No,' Dane said sternly, 'we couldn't. And I'm sure there are things we can do here to help your mother. That's what we should be doing, while she is busy.'

Jonathan fidgeted unenthusiastically. 'Peter always goes away for weekends. I wish we did.'

Eden bit her lip. Saturdays weren't usually much fun for him when she was stuck in the shop and Peter wasn't here for him to play with. 'We always go out on Sundays, though,' she said without thinking.

'Just to Grandma's and it's only for lunch, which isn't much fun,' he muttered.

Eden expected Dane to say something sarcastic and was surprised when he told his son firmly that he wanted to hear no more remarks like that! Then, looking from Jonathan to her, he announced quietly. 'I have a cottage in the country, not too far from town. Why don't we spend the weekend there?'

Jonathan was all for it. 'Whereabouts is it?' he cried excitedly, 'Does it have a garden?'

'It's in Sussex,' Dane replied. 'And, yes, it does have a garden of a kind.'

About to refuse, for it would mean closing the shop again, Eden hesitated. According to Briggs, her mother would be home tomorrow, at the latest, and she would be ringing, inviting them to lunch. Dane wouldn't go, she was certain, and she had no desire to leave him and go by herself. If she went to his cottage, whatever it was like, she would avoid any risk of an embarrassing confrontation with her mother, at least until the following week. Having already had a row with Trevor, she didn't feel like facing the fuss her mother was going to make when she discovered Dane was staying at the flat. That could wait until Monday!

Seeing her still hesitating, Dane asked lightly, 'Can't you make up your mind?'

Eden's cheeks went pink. 'W-what size of cottage did you say you have?'

'I didn't.' He grinned mockingly, 'But don't worry, there's enough room. You won't have to share.'

Missing the point of this conversation entirely, Jonathan begged eagerly. 'Do say you'll come, Mum!' He tugged at her hand, 'Dad and I will look after you. Won't we?' he appealed to Dane.

'It will give us a better chance to get to know each other,' Dane added his persuasions to Jonathan's, but looking so impartially from one to the other that Eden couldn't be sure who he was referring to? 'Think of all the lovely fresh air,' he smiled.

'We can't live on that!' Jonathan chanted automatically, but was so obviously excited that Eden felt obliged to set aside any doubts and give in. After all, if she refused, apart from any other considerations, Dane could probably, quite legitimately take Jonathan off for the weekend by himself? Then where would she be?

CHAPTER EIGHT

THEY left London in the early evening. Dane had taken Jonathan shopping for his TV games then left him with Mrs Willis while he went out to pursue his own business for an hour. From his office, he drove directly to Eden's shop to pick her up, then, after packing a few things at the flat, they set off for Sussex.

Dane had said not to worry about dinner, they could eat on the way. This they did, about seven, with due regard for Jonathan's age. The inn Dane choose was old and shabby, it's appearance giving no hint of the excellence of its food. Jonathan choose French fries with his fish while Eden and Dane had salad and steaks. The desserts were good, too, and again they all went for something different. Dane had apple pie and custard while Eden couldn't resist the chocolate gateau.

She looked at Jonathan's huge strawberry ice-cream covered in gooey syrup and hoped he wouldn't be ill.

'I'm never ill, Mum,' he grinned, as she expressed her doubts aloud. 'You should see what I ate in France.'

Again, when she thought Dane might make use of an opportunity to criticise her parents, he merely smiled and said, 'French cuisine takes some beating. When were you there last, Eden?'

'Not since our honeymoon,' she replied hesitantly. 'I've been meaning to go back but I never seem to have time.'

'Grandma says . . .'

'That's enough, Jonathan.'

'Women!' Jonathan shrugged, and she wondered if this was something he had picked up from Dane, for certainly her father would never dare use such an expression.

She noticed the waitress glancing at Dane with

131

interest and felt her heart tighten. He was worth looking at, she couldn't blame the girl. It wasn't just that he was tall and broad and ruggedly handsome, it was the controlled force about him, the aura of sheer masculinity, that might almost have been visible. In a black, open-necked shirt, that revealed the crisp, dark hairs on his chest, he alluded strength and sexual vitality.

Eden swallowed then flushed as she realised he was watching her watching him. 'Th—that was delicious,' she stammered.

'The meal?' His eyes glinted mockingly. 'Shall we wait and have coffee at the cottage?'

'Yes.' She rose with undue haste, 'A good idea.'

Jonathan protested, wanting more ice-cream but didn't make a fuss when he didn't get any. He was a lovable boy, Eden thought, settling for anything to get her mind off Dane as they set out again. If he didn't behave all the time, and she didn't think she would wish him to, he accepted chastisement, provided it was fair, as part and parcel of his childhood.

From East Grinstead, they travelled through a maze of minor roads before coming on the cottage unexpectedly. Eden wasn't familiar with the area and gazed around with interest. The countryside looked rather lonely and desolate, with wild stretches of common and forest.

'Where are we?' she asked, as Dane turned a blind corner and shot up a lane to stop in front of a house she hadn't even noticed they were approaching.

'I'll show you on a map, later,' he promised.

Eden nodded as she quickly loosened her seat belt, as eager as Jonathan was, behind her, to take a good look at the place. While Dane carried in their luggage, she and Jonathan explored the garden which comprised mostly of an acre of grass running down to a stream. A wide copse of huge trees formed a shelter belt to the east which explained why the house was almost invisible from the road.

The house was much larger than she'd envisaged and she liked the mellow brick-work that blended so well with the landscape. Indoors, were two spacious rooms and a kitchen on the ground floor, while upstairs there were three good-sized bedrooms, one with a bathroom *en suite*, and another bathroom.

'Some cottage!' Eden remarked drily.

'Isn't it,' Dane quirked, showing Jonathan his bedroom. It was tucked away in a corner, up a short flight of steps, and he instantly loved it.

Eden could see how it would appeal to a small boy. It was cosily furnished, and under the eaves, it had an air of secretiveness about it. Jonathan would feel safe and snug here, yet in possession of a privacy that was usually only afforded to grown-ups.

'Can I go to bed now, Mum?' he begged, having eagerly inspected everything.

She wondered if he wouldn't be too excited to sleep but as it was long past his normal bedtime, she agreed. While Dane accompanied him to the bathroom, she found his pyjamas and waited until he returned to tuck him in and kiss him good night. His eyes were already closed as she turned off the light.

'He acts like a deprived child,' she said, suddenly determined that Dane should know he wasn't. She couldn't provide things like country cottages, but weren't items like this just the icing on the cake?

Again Dane surprised her. 'I'd say he doesn't act like a spoiled one. I've known kids who have so much they don't appreciate anything any more.'

At the top of the staircase, she paused. 'Would you mind, Dane, if I had a shower before I made coffee? I hadn't time when we got back from the shop. If I could just have my things?'

'I'll get them,' he nodded. 'They're still downstairs. Shall I put them in the end room?'

It was the one which clearly wasn't his but she didn't know if he was giving her a choice. Lowering her lashes to hide a sudden confusion, she murmured, 'Thank-you.'

She was in the room when he returned with her case and again she was only able to manage a brief word of thanks.

'No trouble,' he shrugged, his eyes moving over her speculatively. 'Just come down when you're ready. There's no hurry.'

The water wasn't very hot as the heater hadn't been on many minutes, but the coolness of the shower revived her better than a hot one might have done. The towels were large and fluffy, the bathroom well appointed. She couldn't help feeling curious about the way Dane lived, the apparent change in his circumstances since they'd been married. His house in Scotland and even this could be company property, but, if it was, his position in the company must be fairly important to command such generosity.

She had packed a long, kaftan style dress in a soft lawn cotton which she put on after brushing her hair into a silky cloud about her shoulders. After fastening the buttons up the front of it, she slipped her bare feet into a pair of light sandals and went downstairs to join him.

She found him in the kitchen, unplugging the percolator. On the table beside him was a tray set with cups and a plate of cheese and biscuits. He glanced around briefly when he heard her, then looked again, a muscle tensing in his jaw. 'All dressed up,' he observed, sounding surprisingly curt.

'Not really,' Eden felt unduly hurt. 'I came down to help, not to be ornamental.'

He let out his breath with a dry smile. 'You probably couldn't help being ornamental if you tried.'

'That kind of insult I can stand,' she quipped back, gazing around her with interest. The kitchen reflected much the same pattern in its basic units as the kitchen at the house in Shetland did. Everything was organised for maximum efficiency of labour, dishwasher, sinks, ovens and hotplates, arranged in almost exactly the same way.

'It's not difficult to see that you supervised the

modernisation of both your houses,' she said. 'The kitchens, anyway, are so similar, it couldn't be a coincidence.'

He put the percolator on the tray. 'By both houses, I presume you mean the one in Scotland?'

'How many do you have?' she exclaimed.

'Ah, that would be telling,' he smiled.

'It's been said that sailors have a wife in every port.'

'Well,' his eyes glinted as he picked up the tray and beckoned for her to follow, 'I find a house more reliable than a wife. At least it can't get up and walk away.'

She deserved that, she supposed, but her eyes were blinded with sudden tears as she trailed behind him. Then she shook her head impatiently. She was used to the sharpness of his tongue which could twist things so swiftly to suit his own purpose. Why let it bother her?

Instead of making for the lounge, as she had expected him to, he strode straight through the open front door. On the roughly slabbed terrace that ran along the front of the house, she saw he had placed a table and a couple of chairs.

'Whenever I come down here in summer, this is where I like to sit, at this time of day.' Placing the tray on the table, he pulled out a chair for her, and if he noticed her tears, he made no comment. He did drop a hand for a second on her shoulder, though, and she felt instinctively this was meant as an apology for hurting her.

Eden looked at him, as he sat beside her, ready to forgive him anything in a rush of gratitude she didn't try and hide. For all his taunts, he must have judged her mood exactly to have thought of this. The view unfolding before them in the fading light, was wild and uncompromising yet strangely soothing, and she knew she needed this peace and quiet, after the last few weeks.

'But not too much of it,' Dane murmured, laughter in his eyes as he expertly interpreted her revealing thoughts.

Eden's grey eyes flashed indignantly. 'I wish you'd stop reading my mind without permission. It's very unnerving.'

'You make it too easy.' He passed her some coffee after putting sugar and cream in it, exactly how she liked it. 'I could see you relaxing, deciding you could live in such splendid isolation forever, but you're much too beautiful to be hidden away and never seen.'

'I'm getting to feel an affinity with such places,' she was suddenly serious. 'It was the same in Shetland. Funny, isn't it?' she grimaced wryly, 'I always thought I was a town bird.'

'My crew, in Shetland, thought you were the best looking bird they had seen.'

She giggled. 'When I wasn't there to defend myself?'

He grinned drily. 'Don't worry, the few who saw you were so loud in their praises, you wouldn't have thought there was any need to.'

She sighed nostalgically. 'I'd like to go back there. Do you think there'd be any trade for antiques?'

'Not hankering after Lawson, are you?'

His abrupt change of subject stabbed her, so she had to wait a moment before she could speak. 'Don't you think I'd have married him years ago, if I had been?'

'You could have been frightened of losing Jonathan . . .'

'It never occurred to me.'

'No?' He stared down at the table, his fingers tapping it, his mouth set. Then he straightened and lay back in his chair, confusingly exchanging his frown for a smile. 'In case you're worrying,' he murmured, 'I've left the door open so we can hear Jonathan if he wakes. I checked, though, while you were in the shower, and he was fast asleep.'

'So did I, before I came down,' Eden said.

'So,' he smiled, 'why don't we relax and enjoy ourselves?' While she was still feeling slightly bewildered by his changing moods, he reached under the table and drew forth an ice bucket, complete with a bottle of wine. 'This should help to cheer us up,' he said drily. 'I thought you might prefer it to brandy with your coffee?'

She looked at it closer. 'Champagne?'

'I don't know if it will go as well,' he admitted with a grin, 'but it seems more in keeping with a summer's night.'

It was delicious and, combined with Dane's company and the silence surrounding them, gave her a wonderful feeling of well-being. All Eden's troubles faded. Nothing seemed worth worrying over, anymore. After three glasses she even found sufficient courage to ask Dane how long he'd had the house?'

'A few years,' he replied idly.

'Company?'

'In a way.' He shrugged, with the evasiveness she found difficult to understand. Not for the first time his attitude puzzled her. She had been bracing herself for an inquisition over Trevor but, apart from the few questions he had already asked, he didn't mention any of the things he must have gleaned from the conversation he had overheard at the shop. As always, he seemed intent on distancing himself from anything that had happened in the past. She could have sworn he had been desperate to know every detail of her confinement in hospital, with Jonathan, but for some reason wouldn't allow himself to ask. And there was a kind of wariness about him which prevented her from raising the subject herself.

It was dark when a light wind blew up, bringing with it a spatter of rain. 'We'd better retire,' Dane said with a rueful grin.

'Oh, no!' Eden cried as the rain almost immediately grew heavier, 'It can't be a wet weekend!'

'The forecast's good.' Dane began loading things on the tray. 'We often get the odd shower, with all the rivers around. It's nothing to panic about.'

She followed him inside, smothering a yawn. For the past hour they had only been talking occasionally—she must have been falling asleep.

In the hall, he told her to stand still while he put on the light. 'We don't want you crashing around and hurting yourself, or wakening Jonathan.'

'It might take an earthquake to do that,' she laughed. 'The first year of his life, I don't think he slept at all but he's certainly made up for it since.'

Dane seemed a long time in finding the light switch. Even then he didn't look at her but kept his eyes fixed on the load he was carrying. 'Shut the door, will you?' he asked tersely, 'while I dispose of this.'

The lock was stiff and he was back while she was still struggling with it. Moving her firmly aside, he turned the key with his stronger fingers. 'Doesn't get enough use,' he grunted.

'How often are you here?' she asked.

'Not often enough.'

His abruptness discouraged her, making her stumble. She might have fallen if his arm hadn't shot out to save her. She felt him stiffen and draw a short breath as he attempted to put her from him, but when he started to let her go, she swayed towards him involuntarily. The wine she had drank was making her dizzy and all sensible, coherent thought was being swamped by a flood of physical desire sweeping through her. Never had she wanted to be kissed so much. Never had she wanted Dane to make love to her as much. Lately she had felt she was existing on a barren plain, now she knew why.

'Dane——' she whispered, raising her lips to meet the descending fierceness of his.

Immediately she was lost in the ravaging possession of his mouth. Yet, as he kissed her, she was aware of some part of him still fighting her. He didn't like how she tempted him and a thirst for revenge might have been reflected in the ruthless tightness of the arms which suddenly went around her. Shudders of potent desire flowed from her breasts to her thighs as her hands clutched at his broad, muscular shoulders. She could feel a tension in his body that almost frightened her but the knowledge that he wanted her spurred her on and she pressed closer.

'Eden!' Her name sounded wrenched from his lips as he suddenly picked her up and made towards the darkened staircase. He seemed to take the stairs two at a time in his haste to reach the bedroom.

On his wide bed, his mouth crushed hers again and a few frantic moments divested them of their clothes. She could feel his control slipping, along with her own, as they devoured the perfection of each other's bodies.

'Please kiss me,' she whispered and he hesitated only a moment before coming down on her with a smothered oath, his weight crushing her into the mattress as he pressed his mouth passionately to her pleading one.

He kissed her savagely until her head was reeling, her body tormented by longing. She shuddered at the burning contact of their bare limbs and moved in mindless ecstasy against him, which inflamed his already impatient senses.

They made love quickly and urgently, the chemistry between them explosive, their bodies fitting together like two connecting parts of a puzzle. She accepted the driving force of his passion with a kind of fierce joy rising up inside her. It wasn't something she could easily contain and her gasping cries of pleasure mingled with his hoarser ones.

They rode the crest of the storm together, with the prospect of limitless sensation driving them frantically onwards. Waves of thunderous pleasure enveloped them, tossing them higher and higher until their goal was reached, the ultimate force of it making their bodies shudder violently beneath it's awesome climax.

It was mind-shattering. Eden clung to him afterwards, not wishing to let him go. 'You don't know what you do to me!' she breathed shakily.

He kissed her gently. 'I have a very good idea. You do the same to me.'

Did she? Eden wondered hazily. It was possible Dane was speaking the truth but wanting each other could mean different things to both of them.

'No other woman,' he began, then abruptly cut himself off by kissing her again, just as she was getting interested. It was no time for retrospection, though. Already her starved body was clamouring for more and she could tell by the darkening of his eyes as he raised his head slightly to look at her, that he was getting the message loud and clear, and responding to it.

They made love again, slowly this time, their hands and lips exploring each other, taking their time. His mouth made paths all over her, lingering on her breasts and flat stomach, the soft skin of her inner thighs. Then she was lost in a world spinning again with sexual excitement, which mounted with increasing intensity each time he possessed her. When the spinning eventually stopped, they were completely spent and remained entwined long after the tension had left their bodies and they fell asleep.

Eden noticed the sun was shining when she stirred in Dane's arms again. He was awake and staring down at her as he leaned over her with an intimacy that warmed her all over. Yet before she could reach up and kiss him, he drew away with what could only be described as a jerk.

'Dane . . .?' she tried not to sound hurt.

Swinging his long legs to the floor, he reached for the robe flung carelessly over a nearby chair. It was short and black and it made Eden shiver as hard to see him in it as it did when he was naked.

Ignoring her plea, he said shortly. 'I'll have a shower and start breakfast while you're getting up.'

She frowned, a little of her happiness evaporating. 'What time is it, for heaven's sake?'

'Almost eight,' he replied, like it was midday!

The bathroom door closed and she heard the shower running. He had taken a pair of shorts with him and he came out wearing them, with a thin body shirt. She gulped at the sight of his long, bare legs.

'Dane . . .' she tried again.

'Don't be long,' he said, sparing her merely a brief glance as he strode from the room.

Would she ever understand him! Deciding in her bewilderment to use the other bathroom, she tossed back the sheets and used her dress as a dressing-gown until she could find her jeans. When she was ready, she went to wake Jonathan but he was sleeping so soundly she decided to leave him. Another hour wouldn't do him any harm as he had been tired last night.

She found Dane in the kitchen, their breakfast nearly ready. 'I'm getting lazy,' she said. 'You should have waited for me.'

'If I had we might have been having breakfast at lunchtime,' he quipped. 'You had too much champagne.'

She stared at him, wounded. 'You don't think . . .'

He didn't allow her to continue. 'Shut up, there's a good girl. My thoughts aren't for publication, this morning.' He poured her orange juice and broke eggs into a pan. She saw bacon and sausages under the grill.

She made an effort to co-operate. 'Where on earth has it all come from?' she asked in amazement.

'I sent one of the girls from the office out shopping to Harrods, yesterday, then packed it all in ice boxes. Usually I get someone to fill the deep freeze if I'm going to be in London any length of time and can get down here often.'

Eden, keeping her hurt resolutely at the back of her mind, could imagine coming regularly to the cottage with Dane and Jonathan. Then she thought of coming with Dane, alone, and tried to prevent her imagination from conjuring up erotic pictures of the two of them spending the weekend in bed. She gulped down her juice quickly and took the empty glass to the sink.

As soon as she got near him, with her blood on fire from tumultuous thoughts, she couldn't resist slipping her arms around him as he stood frying the eggs. Pressing her head against his shoulder, she murmured, 'You haven't kissed me, this morning.'

'Haven't I?' Suddenly he turned, startling her by grabbing her and holding her tightly while his mouth swooped to take possession of hers. He kissed her until they were both trembling. Long before he stopped her heart was racing furiously.

When he raised his head and she stared up at him, he gazed down at her, his eyes smouldering. 'You see how dangerous kissing can be? With us it's a form of instant ignition. Which wouldn't matter if we could spend the rest of the day alone together.'

Eden drew a sharp breath. She and Dane were discovering how perfectly attuned they were physically, the only problem was they were beginning to want each other all the time. So many questions hovered on the tip of her tongue but she sensed she would be wasting her time to ask even one of them. Dane was not answering questions at the moment, not even those he was asking himself. If only he would suggest something even semi-permanent, such as living together, she might be able to judge where she stood with him, but this blank wall of silence he erected between them left her with a sense of frustration she couldn't fight.

She tried to joke about it, forcing a smile to her lips. 'It's not a day for lazing in bed, is it?'

'I wouldn't be lazing!' he grinned, turning back to his pan but obviously attempting to match her mood. 'However, as soon as Jonathan gets up we will go out and get some fresh air. It may do us more good.'

'It didn't do me much good last night,' she pretended to grumble as she accepted a plate of bacon and eggs.

Dane eyed her grimly as he joined her at the table with about everything on his plate, she noted sourly, but the kitchen sink! 'You drank too much champagne.'

She eyed him indignantly over the rim of her glass of orange juice. Did he have to keep reminding her! 'You would have felt insulted if I hadn't. It was you, if you remember, who kept filling me up.'

Dane's mouth twisted wryly but before he could reply, Jonathan appeared, still in his pyjamas, sounding as indignant as Eden had done, half an hour ago. 'Why didn't someone wake me? I want to go outside.'

His pyjamas had bears all over them and Dane teased. 'You'd better not go out dressed like that. The wolves around here don't care for bears.'

'My bears are very friendly,' Jonathan said earnestly. 'But I'll wear my jeans, like Mum.'

Eden laughed and took him back upstairs to find them then came down with him again, after he dressed. Later they took a picnic, which they ate beside a rocky outcrop, near some trees, several hours later.

It was an ideal day and they walked for miles over the Ashdown Forest. Dane didn't change out of his shorts but he did put on a pair of thick, knee length socks to protect his legs from the roughness of the heath. He made an ideal father, Eden thought, listening to him explaining the area to Jonathan as they went along. This was apparently one of the last remaining tracts of the huge Wealden forest of Anderida, which in Roman times stretched for 120 miles in a broad swathe across south-east England. The massive oaks were felled for the furnaces of the great Sussex iron industry in the early 17th century, the forest ponds, which were damned to drive the forge hammers, still a distinctive part of the Sussex scenery. Today, Dane said, the forest was split up into separate patches of woodland and moorland in which were the sources of many rivers including the Ouse, the Arun and the Rother. Ashdown was the largest of these patches but he liked others, further west. The forests of St Leonard's, Balcombe, Tilgate and Worth, he told them, were once the haunts of smugglers, highwaymen and cattle thieves and, especially in winter, could be wild, lonely places.

Eden, always full of vitality, was a good walker, but Jonathan's shorter legs grew tired. When he complained, Dane swung him up on his broad shoulders and Eden's heart contracted at the sight of the tall, powerfully built man swinging along with the small boy as if he was no weight at all.

By the time they stopped for lunch Jonathan was quite recovered and began climbing trees to try and

spot highwaymen while Eden unpacked their sandwiches.

'It's lovely here,' she smiled, 'and so quiet. We've
scarcely seen a soul.'

Dane glanced at her as he stretched out lazily by her
side. 'That's probably because I'm familiar with the less
frequented paths but there is enough space for it never
to seem crowded even when there are plenty people
about.'

Eden nodded. 'But I still like Shetland.'

He laughed. 'You've really fallen for the Shetlands,
haven't you?'

'Yes, although . . .' she had been about to say that
anywhere would seem good if he were there, but
changed it quickly to, 'there are other places.'

Jonathan came down the tree for a sandwich and a
can of pop. 'Can we go back there with you, Dad?' he
asked, proving that children have big ears.

'We will see,' Dane stuck firmly to the non-committal
answer he had given before and began talking to him
about other things.

If only she were as easily diverted, Eden thought
ruefully. She slept for an hour after they finished eating
and Dane woke her with a kiss. 'I've always wanted to
awaken Sleeping Beauty,' he murmured, a teasing glint
in his eye. 'At school they would never let me play the
part. They had the nerve to say I was too big.'

'How old were you?' she asked sleepily, finding it
easy to smile with lips warm from his kiss.

'Jonathan's age.'

She giggled, unable to imagine him, even at six, in
silks and satins and tottering heels. She was giggling so
hard that as she got to her feet, she stumbled against
him and his arms shot automatically around her.
Bending his mouth to her cheek, he muttered huskily.
'I'm surprised you make a habit of doing this, especially
when you know the consequences.'

'Maybe I don't mind,' she whispered.

This time when he kissed her, it wasn't a gentle kiss

and she felt her nipples harden under the thin top she wore as they pressed against his chest. 'Witch!' he muttered, his hand curving her chin, his thumb brushing her lips which his mouth had been reluctant to leave. 'Wait until this evening.'

Eden felt like singing as they wandered homewards, his threats acting more potently than the strongest wine. She refused to look beyond the weekend, which promised to be wonderful.

Jonathan had peanut-butter sandwiches and an apple when they got back to the cottage while she and Dane had toast spread with honey. They decided to keep the luscious cream gateau Dane had bought to have with their dinner.

While Dane took Jonathan out to explore the garden, Eden prepared the chicken and put it in the oven. A ready stuffed chicken and frozen vegetables wasn't exactly *cordon bleu* but, as Dane pointed out, he hadn't planned that they should spend the entire weekend in the kitchen. Nevertheless, glancing around the cosy apartment, Eden knew an urge to start baking. She could imagine making cakes and pastries in a kitchen like this on a winter's afternoon, waiting for the two men in her life to come home, one from business, the other from school.

So much for the shop or the career she had always wanted but never had. If she could choose, she would give it all up and settle for being Dane's wife. It might mean living for years in remote places but, for the first time in her life she felt she had got her values right. And she could always write a book about antiques or give talks about them, if he was busy and she had time to spare?

Then she impatiently thrust such a dream from her mind as one that had little chance of coming true, as she heard them coming into the hall. It didn't do to read too much into Dane's new warmth and friendliness. Sometime in the near future he might be presenting her with a plan for sharing Jonathan. Yesterday, when he was supposed to be in his office, he had probably been consulting his solicitor? When she thought how she might be in danger of losing not only him but Jonathan, tears of anguish rushed to her eyes.

'I want to damn the stream, Mum!' Jonathan burst into the kitchen. 'Dad says he doesn't mind if you don't?'

Eden had turned quickly to the oven, yanking open the door in order to hide her sudden distress. The waves of heat that met her, combined with Jonathan's boisterous presence, did the trick. She was able to swing around and look at them with at least some composure and an excuse for the heightened colour in her cheeks. 'I don't see why not,' she agreed. 'It was something I always wanted to do, at your age.'

'I take it you weren't allowed to?' Dane remarked drily.

Her mother would have had a fit, her nursemaid instantly dismissed. 'Something like that,' she shrugged.

Eden went with them to watch but soon, to Dane's amusement, she left him sitting on the bank while she rolled up the bottoms of her jeans and joined Jonathan. The stream was wide and though shallow was impossible to damn satisfactorily with the few stones available, and the sandy mud they dredged from it's bed to use as cement kept getting washed away. In the end, they gave up and settled for paddling. Then, in no time, it seemed, Dane was announcing that, as it was well after seven, he would go and put the vegetables on.

'Oh, heavens!' Eden scrambled out of the stream in alarm, 'The chicken!'

'I've just checked. It will take about half an hour, but you'd better get under the shower—both of you,' he threatened, his dancing eyes on Eden's mud-spattered face. 'You can use mine, Eden, then come and help in the kitchen.'

Jonathan went to bed soon after dinner, not because he was sent but because he was so tired after the days activities, he could scarcely keep his eyes open.

'About time!' Dane growled, pulling Eden into his arms when she returned from putting him to bed, to help with the dishes, which she saw he had coped with admirably by piling them into the dishwasher!

'I'm sure Jonathan wouldn't be alarmed if he saw you kissing me,' she murmured with rosy cheeks.

'There are kisses and kisses.' He began pressing urgent ones over her face and mouth. 'The trouble is, I forget when to stop.'

She laughed, pushing away from him, but her own eyes were as warm as his as she rubbed the sensitive skin on her neck where his lips had lingered. 'Can we have our coffee outside again?' she asked demurely. 'I'd like to see the sunset.'

'You may be lucky!' he warned, and as his voice menaced softly, her whole body tingled with delightful anticipation.

She slept in Dane's bed again that night and they spent the next day pottering about the house and lounging in the garden. The weather was so glorious that Jonathan was content to play in the stream. When he grew tired of this he pretended to be a Red Indian in the woods, while Eden luxuriated in the sunshine and Dane's companionship.

He didn't talk much but he was there and she was able to feast her eyes on him. In the afternoon, when he stopped doing odd jobs and fell asleep by her side, she had a field day!

All too soon it was time to leave for London. They decided to wait until after dinner, when the roads would be quieter, but they didn't linger too late, for Jonathan's sake.

'Why can't we stay longer?' Jonathan complained. 'If you have to go to the shop, Mum, couldn't Dad stop with me?'

Eden paled, not so much at what he had said but because it made her realise how completely he had accepted his father and might not be reluctant to spend some time with him, away from her.

Dane glanced at her sharply and saved her from replying by explaining firmly, though not unkindly. 'I have to get back too, son. I'm not officially on holiday, you see.'

As he had been called to the 'phone several times during the weekend, on business, Jonathan accepted this with a boyish grimace of repugnance. 'Okay, Dad, but can we come back?'

'We will have to think about it,' Dane gave his standard reply but Eden noticed his mouth tighten as he began carrying their luggage out to the car. As he passed her, his face was so curiously blank that somehow she felt convinced that they wouldn't be. She had a sinking feeling, as she said a silent goodbye to the cottage and the nights she had spent in Dane's arms, that, as far as Dane was concerned, this one weekend had somehow served its purpose.

CHAPTER NINE

THE following morning, Eden woke feeling miserable. For a moment she lay, unable to immediately grasp where she was, aware only of a black feeling of depression. It was seven o'clock and Monday, the beginning of another working week, but she was sure it wasn't just this. Then she remembered she had slept on her own again. Dane had gone out as soon as they had returned last night, and hadn't come back until long after she had given up waiting for him and gone to bed. It had been well after midnight before he had returned and he hadn't disturbed her. She had heard him go quietly to his room and close the door.

She had wanted to go to him, to demand to know where he had been? If he had been seeing another woman? She couldn't believe he would go straight from her to someone else but she was so upset that her mind had been alive with suspicion. It was more likely that he had stayed out late deliberately, to demonstrate by actions, rather than embarrassing words, that the intimacy between them over the weekend, was not to continue in London.

Her theory seemed proved to be correct, when he didn't get up for breakfast. There was no sound from his room and she couldn't bring herself to risk a further rebuff by knocking on his door and asking if he would like a cup of tea? Without seeing him, she took a protesting Jonathan to play with Peter, after giving Jennifer a ring to ascertain that it would be all right. Then she set off for the shop alone.

Dane called for her around six and when she glanced at him coolly, he apologised blandly for being late. 'Jonathan and I took Peter and his mother to the zoo. Jennifer and I could hardly drag the boys away.'

Eden knew she went pale and she blinked with dismay as she stared at him. Wrenching her eyes from his watchful ones, she grabbed her bag and hurried Jonathan from the premises. 'That was good of you,' she smiled, without counting the cost to stiff face muscles. 'Jonathan loves going there.'

'Dad and Mrs Graham were talking so hard they missed the elephants!' Jonathan giggled.

Before you could miss something as big as that, you had to be absorbed! As Eden's suspicions began running riot again, she clamped down on them mercilessly. 'I expect they've both seen elephants before,' she observed lightly.

Dane whistled softly between his teeth, irritating her both by this and by not saying anything. His silence seemed an insult to her intelligence! Occasionally he took to task an offending fellow motorist but his mood was too good, apparently, for him to lose his temper completely. Like a lesser mortal, like herself felt like doing! Eden thought morosely.

They hadn't been home five minutes before the telephone rang. 'Yes?' Eden snapped.

'Good gracious!' exclaimed her mother. 'You do sound grumpy!'

'I'm sorry, Mother,' Eden retorted, in more normal tones. 'I've just got in and I'm tired, not in the mood for idle conversation, anyway.'

'Aren't you going to ask how I enjoyed my holiday?'

'You always do, Mother. I take it for granted . . .'

'My goodness, you do seem irritable!' Irene paused then continued smoothly. 'The company you're keeping doesn't appear to be doing much for you. Have you still got your lodger?'

How did she know about that? 'Dane is not a lodger, Mother!'

'Sorry, darling,' Irene said, too quickly. 'Of course not. But I'm not sure what to call him, I admit.'

Eden was sure she could guess what her mother would like to call him! But if Irene was behaving badly,

maybe so was she? Yet how could she be friendly when
Irene's obvious intention was to separate her from
Dane, undoubtedly with Trevor's assistance! Eden
wasn't fooled, she was merely curious as to what
lengths her mother was prepared to go to, to achieve
this.

'I'll have to go now,' she said.

'Oh, wait a moment!' Irene wailed, 'I wanted to
remind you about my annual party for charity on
Wednesday. I've been trying to get hold of you all
weekend. I know you don't like my ringing you at the
shop and I thought you might have forgotten?'

Eden had. It had gone clean out of her head. Every
year, at this time, Irene, with the aid of friends,
organised a dress show and buffet, the proceeds going
to charity. Sometimes she bullied one or two well
known artists into performing. Irene was good at that
kind of thing, Eden thought drily, even if she also
bullied others into doing most of the work.

'What night is it?' she asked cautiously.

'I've just told you—Wednesday. And bring Dane,'
her mother purred. 'I know he would wish to contribute
by buying two tickets for such a good cause, and don't
bother Mrs Willis to baby sit. Jonathan can sleep here.'

'I'll see,' was all the promise Eden gave, as she rang off.

'Anyone I know?' Dane asked idly from the kitchen
doorway. 'Good job we have unbreakable 'phones.'

Are they? she wondered blankly. 'Mother,' she
muttered.

'Want something, does she?'

'Us!' Eden retorted tersely, explaining about the
party without mentioning Irene's jibes over him staying
here. He would get to know what Irene thought of that
soon enough, if they were to meet again.

'It sounds—fun.'

Maybe he had been right to hesitate over his choice
of words. She had her own reservations, too. Namely,
that charity wasn't wholly what Irene had in mind.
'Would you like to come with me?'

He gazed at her steadily. 'If you want me to? Your parents are, after all, as we've both said, Jonathan's grandparents.'

Not his future in-laws—he wouldn't say that! She looked at him bleakly. 'The tickets are twenty-five pounds a head and everyone is expected to pay over the odds.'

'I think I could just about manage.'

'I thought I should warn you.'

'Thanks.'

Did he have to sound so derisive—but, then, did she feel it necessary to suggest so ridiculously that twenty-five pounds might be beyond him? Unhappily she muddled on. 'Mother always believes she is acting for the best but not everyone is of the same opinion. You don't have to go.'

'Leave it, Eden,' he said coolly. 'If I haven't enjoyed visiting your parents in the past, I'm sure one more time won't kill me.'

Feeling rebuffed, Eden shrugged and went on her way to the shower. Dinner could wait! Perhaps if Dane was hungry he would regret speaking to her so sharply! She caught a glimpse of Jonathan watching TV as she passed the living-room door and suddenly the flat she had once felt so proud of seemed small and cramped compared with what Dane could offer him. She banged her bedroom door tersely, then halted abruptly. What was the matter with her? The flat was small but what of it? It wasn't so much the size of a house, was it? It was the happiness generating within that was important!

As she showered, she wondered desperately what her mother was up to? She had scarcely mentioned Jonathan who was usually her main topic of conversation. Which suggested she was concentrating on someone else, and that someone else could only be Dane? Once Irene got rid of him, she could relax and get back to her daughter and grandson again, but how could she begin doing this at a party? Perhaps in this instance, Eden brooded, she was being unduly

suspicious? Irene didn't sound antagonistic and she
would know better than to imagine she could show
Dane up in a bad light. She wouldn't have forgotten
that neither his appearance or manner were anything to
be ashamed of. There could be other ways of getting at
him, though. Irene was an expert when it came to
barbed digs, cleverly cloaked by charming smiles, but
then she would know that Dane was no helpless
adversary, who couldn't give as good as he got. Eden
sighed as she turned off the water and wrapped her wet
body in a large towel. It was no use becoming paranoid
over it, she would just have to wait and see. Dane was
quite able to look after himself and she was probably
sensing danger where none existed. It wasn't until days
after the party that she realised her mother was much
more ingenious than she had ever given her credit for.

Dane didn't go out that evening but he may well have
done because of the distance he put between them. He
was pleasant enough over dinner but a remoteness
about him suggested the barriers were up again. Having
taken the initiative before, Eden dared not even try and
cross them. This time it was up to Dane. If anything
came of what they had now, it must be because he
wanted it as much as she did. One of these days, she
was aware, he could simply disappear from her life and
she might never see him again, but she knew she would
never derive any lasting peace or happiness from
influencing him into staying with her.

When they were eating breakfast, the following
morning, he asked what she intended wearing for the
party?

'Why not let me buy you a new dress?' he offered
with a smile. 'I feel I owe you, both for looking after me
in Shetland and letting me stay here.'

'It would be terrible, wouldn't it,' she taunted
bitterly, 'if you had to leave feeling you were in my
debt? Haven't you forgotten all the lifts you give me to
work, to say nothing of all the other contributions
you've made, including a free weekend . . .'

'Eden!' he interrupted gently, though his eyes were harder than his voice. 'I merely wanted to give you something, a present if you like. But you must know I owe you far more than you owe me.'

'I'm sorry,' she stammered, her blue-grey eyes suddenly pleading forgiveness, 'I didn't mean to sound ungrateful but I don't really need a new dress. And, if I did, I'm quite capable of buying one for myself.'

'Just as you like,' he replied curtly, draining his coffee cup so she couldn't tell what he was thinking. 'Now, if you're ready, I'd like to go. I'm late enough as it is.'

Numbly Eden got her things together and joined him in the car. He dropped her off on his way to his office. Jonathan was staying with Mrs Willis until he returned for lunch. All morning she wondered if she had been wrong in refusing to let him buy her a dress? She hadn't been altogether truthful when she had said she didn't need one. Strictly speaking, she may not, but the white one she had worn when she had dined with him was the best she had and years old. When she had gone out with Trevor it hadn't worried her that she wasn't dressed in the height of fashion. Unconsciously she might have hoped her lack of style would discourage him? Besides, she'd never made enough to spend on clothes for herself, not after Jonathan, the flat and Mrs Willis had been budgeted for. It wouldn't have hurt her to have sunk her pride for once. Recalling the definite coldness in Dane's eyes as he had driven off along the street, she realised it might certainly have been worth it.

This was brought home to her even more forcibly when, later in the day, she discovered he had again taken Jennifer out for the afternoon, with the two boys, and they'd all had tea together. Jennifer's attitude, when she popped around to the flat that evening, to borrow some sugar, was little less than proprietorial, and though Eden did her best to give the impression that she didn't care, she felt so eaten up with jealousy that she feared it might be noticeable?

As a small concession to her guilty conscience over

the dress, she made an appointment to have her hair
done for the party. The Farndales, however, brought
her a load of stuff, that morning, which was all to
unpack and price, while anything in need of attention
had to be taken upstairs. Fortunately Leo offered to
finish off and look after the shop for an hour after
lunch while she was out, which saved her from having
to close it.

It was a long time since she'd had her hair done
professionally and she was amazed at the difference it
made. It rioted like pale gold silk over her small,
shapely head, making her look, she thought, quite
attractive. It even managed to make her white dress
appear reasonably presentable, not as if it had been
washed half a dozen times, she assured herself
anxiously. Later, though, when Dane complimented her
on her appearance, his continuing coldness and the hint
of impatience in his eyes, suggested that his brief
felicitations had been prompted more from politeness
than approval.

Eden glanced at him uncertainly. 'You aren't still
angry because I didn't let you buy me a new dress?'

'Of course not,' he replied indifferently. 'In fact, I
realise how you look has nothing to do with me, and, in
your own way, I suppose, you were letting me know
this. Naturally, if I marry again, I will expect my wife to
dress impeccably for the kind of thing we are attending
this evening, otherwise, what a girl like you chooses to
wear is of no importance to me!'

His words, though casually spoken, hit Eden like
blows, making her flinch. She went white and excused
herself, muttering something about having forgotten a
handkerchief as she dashed back to her room to try and
pull herself together. Closing the door, she leaned
against it, taking deep breaths in order to stem her
tears. She had asked for that, maybe deserved it, but
she could never have guessed it would hurt as much!
Her chest was tight with pain and every steadying
breath she took hurt her throat. Dane had let her know

exactly where she stood with him, and her whole being ached with compounded misery.

Returning to the hall, with a miraculously composed face, Eden was doubly relieved that he didn't even glance in her direction. He was sorting through a handful of keys. Jonathan wasn't coming. It didn't make sense to take him when he would have had to go straight to bed and probably be disturbed by the noise of the party. Mrs Willis had agreed to stay and keep an eye on him again.

As they sped towards the outskirts of the city, Eden sat shivering as a little of her hard won composure dissolved, but if Dane noticed he gave no indication. He was escorting her but the atmosphere between them was so stiff, they might have been strangers.

After ten minutes silence, he asked curtly, 'Is Jennifer never invited to your mother's social evenings?'

Eden hid her increasing jealousy along with the rest of her misery. 'Jennifer hasn't met Mother. Anyway, she has her own friends. It was nice of you to take her out with the boys, though,' she made herself add, 'I could see she appreciated it.'

Dane shot her a sideways glance, his face darkening bleakly as he lapsed into silence again.

Something was bothering him, probably Jennifer? Eden's nerves began screaming in protest but she didn't dare say anything. Instead she murmured unhappily, 'We'll have to talk about Jonathan soon, Dane.'

'Can't wait to get everything cut and dried, can you?'

She swallowed at his grim tone. 'I—just thought it would be best for both of us,' she said haltingly.

'Okay, but not tonight,' he retorted shortly. 'I feel like enjoying myself, for a change. These past few weeks haven't been picnic, exactly.'

How did she reply to that? It wasn't the first time he had mentioned it. The things he was saying made Eden feel she was in front of a firing squad and mortally wounded. Where had she gone wrong? Or had she been wrong all along and never realised? She thought she

recognised in his terseness, a return of his old
symptoms. He was beginning to feel hemmed in and
fighting it.

'It doesn't change much,' Dane remarked, as they
swung into her parents' drive. There was a large paved
area to the side of the imposing house. Briggs was
directing a stream of traffic towards this but when he
spotted Eden and Dane he waved them into a reserved
space at the front of the house.

'I never expected to receive VIP treatment,' Dane
grunted drily, as he manoeuvred into it.

Eden didn't reply. Irene was looking out for them, at
least that was how it seemed. After Eden kissed her
briefly, she tilted her scented cheek for Dane to do the
same. She's up to something! Eden stared at her
suspiciously, wishing she could wring it out of her. She
knew her mother! She was never this nice unless she was
after something.

'So lovely to see you again, Dane,' she heard Irene
pretending. 'I see you haven't brought Jonathan with
you, I suppose it's just as well not to upset his routine.
Children are creatures of habit, don't you think?'

Dane nodded with a slight smile, appearing to be
more absorbed in studying her intently. 'You're looking
well, Irene, not a day older.'

Irene's beauty salon saw to that. She smiled at Dane
brilliantly, obviously appreciating his compliments.
Whereas in the past, his extremely presentable appearance had irritated her, now it seemed to afford her great
satisfaction. Eden bit her lip in frustration as Dane and
her mother skirmished lightly around each other. Just
what was going on? Or what did Irene think she had
going on? What kind of scheme was she devising?

'The fashion show begins in a few minutes,' Irene
announced, while Eden was still wondering. No word of
Trevor, not even a hint! 'You'd better grab a seat, my
dears. There's a buffet, afterwards, and a small cabaret
show someone's managed to put together. Oh, and
dancing! It's been a great effort,' this to Dane.

'Sometimes I wish I had a shop to retreat to, like Eden.
Then I'd be able to produce a plausible excuse for
avoiding having to organise things like this. Of course
we all know how devoted Eden is to her shop, how she
could never bear to part with it. Not that,' she
hastened, 'anyone would be heartless enough to ask her
to. It was her idea, not mine, you know,' she informed
Dane wistfully. 'But we forgave her when we realised
how much the shop and Jonathan were coming to mean
to her.'

She drifted off, leaving Eden almost having to run to
keep up with Dane as he strode through the house,
heading for the huge marquee on the main lawn. She
hadn't time to ponder on what Irene had been babbling
on about. All that nonsense about the shop! Well, she
was fond of it, but not that fond. And it wasn't as if it
was something Dane didn't already know about. He
had probably been bored stiff throughout the entire
discourse, if his impassive face had hidden this politely.

The marquee was full and to Eden's dismay, she and
Dane got parted. She found herself sitting at a table
with some people she didn't recognise.

After a brief speech from one of the organisers,
commenting on the notable achievements of the charity
they were supporting, the audience was thanked and the
show commenced. The models glided expertly back-
wards and forwards. Most of them were professionals,
working for the fashion houses whose clothes were
being displayed. The clothes reflected the brilliance of
their designers and really deserved the increasing
volume of appreciation they received. Eden glanced
down at her own dress and sighed despondently. No
wonder Dane had been so disapproving!

She wondered if he was ashamed of her, too? but this
didn't stop her from going and searching for him as
soon as the show was over. A part of the marquee
which had been partitioned off was opened and people
were helping themselves to the generous buffet and
plentiful supply of coffee and wine available. Most

people carried it back to the tables, now discreetly rearranged around the edge of the floor to allow for dancing.

Eden couldn't see Dane, tall as he was, but suddenly Trevor was at her elbow.

'Hello, darling,' he smiled.

She felt like shouting at him, she was so angry that he had the nerve to approach her so brazenly, sliding an arm around her shoulders as though they were old friends. But hadn't Trevor always been like that, never taking no for an answer? He would consider this latest setback only a temporary disadvantage, any loss of face merely as lost ground, soon to be made up. But if he was relying on her bad memory or forgiving nature, he was about to discover his mistake!

Shaking off his arm, she hissed, 'I told you I don't wish to see you again!'

'You were angry, darling.' He bent over her with an understanding smile. 'Maybe rightly so, I won't deny it, but you have to believe I was acting for what I thought was your own good. You have to admit I must have been when you consider my years of devotion. Compare my record, for instance,' he hesitated before the sparks in her eyes, 'with that of others.'

Naturally he was referring to Dane. Trevor's courage might have failed him at the last moment but it wasn't difficult to guess. Where was Dane, anyway? Taking another quick look around, she saw him deep in conversation with another man. 'I must go,' she mumbled to Trevor, fearing if she lost sight of Dane she might not see him again.

Hastily she dodged through the crowd to his side, careless of the forbidding expression on his face as he glanced up at her approach. As the man he was talking to turned, she recognised him as a well known racing driver. Dane introduced them curtly as she slipped a hand through his arm.

'Your—wife?'

'Not now,' Dane replied tersely. 'We are divorced.'

'I didn't even know you'd been married, old man. Nice to meet you, Mrs Sutherland.' Tony Cook's eyes glinted with sudden interest as they rested on Eden, 'I . . .'

'The cabaret's beginning,' Dane broke in. 'Shall we go and sit down, Eden?'

The other man faded from sight as Dane practically dragged her towards an empty table. 'I didn't mean to intrude,' she gulped, believing this was why he was angry. 'I just didn't think.'

'Nothing to worry about,' he retorted shortly, 'but you're safer away from men like that.'

Eden frowned. All men appeared to present monumental hazards as far as she was concerned! Her bottom lip trembled as she muttered unhappily. 'I sat through the mannequin parade myself.'

'I thought I saw you talking to Lawson?'

Raising her fair head, she gazed at him, suddenly disconcerted. 'That was afterwards, and I wasn't talking to him.'

'Listening, then?'

Averting her eyes, Eden stared blindly at the stage, hearing the first singer being introduced and wishing she had never come. Who would have missed her? She had lost touch with most of her mother's friends and few of them had made any effort to keep in touch with her, especially since their ways weren't hers anymore.

'I only stayed with Trevor long enough to confirm what I told him the other day!' she said fiercely. 'That I have no wish to see him again.'

When Dane didn't answer, she saw his attention had been drawn to the singer and he hadn't heard a word she was saying. The girl was good, Eden could almost forgive her for arousing Dane's interest. She watched as the girl descended from the stage and began wending her way through the tables in the manner of a true professional. Her voice was low and husky and her voluptuous body undulated sensuously but Eden blinked in astonishment when she paused right in front of Dane. For several moments they stared into each other's eyes, as she seemed to be singing for him alone and when, with a seductive smile she moved on, Dane turned, his eyes following her as she returned to the stage.

Eden suddenly felt terribly cold. You couldn't miss instant attraction when it was staring you in the face, could you? Clare Renor was one of the most popular vocalists around. How on earth had she been persuaded to come here? Eden tried desperately to recall what she knew of her. What was it she had just read? Then she remembered. A few weeks ago the papers had been full of Miss Renor's divorce. There had been something connected with the divorce too, something unusual. Eden wished she could remember what it was?

The girl was beautiful, dark, with a slender, enticing figure. Eden glanced at Dane, conscious of his absorption. The cold feeling increased. Was it just the girl's singing, or was he attracted physically, as well? Clare Renor—it was coming back slowly, had something of a reputation as a man-eater, though it was rumoured that she preferred millionaires.

When the song was over, Irene, to Eden's surprise, brought Miss Renor to their table and introduced her.

'You must meet my daughter, my dear, my only child.' Irene smiled sadly, giving the impression that she would have liked a dozen children when she hadn't even wanted one! 'And Dane Sutherland, who used to be her husband. Isn't it wonderful how couples get divorced, today, and still remain friends?'

Miss Renor smiled at Eden coldly, it was clearly Dane she was interested in. As he rose to his feet, her eyes feasted on the animal like elegance of his powerful body beneath the black evening suit. 'Mrs Spencer has been telling me you work for Burford Oils, Mr Sutherland. My cousin ...'

'He is Burford Oils, my dear.' Irene patted Dane's arm complacently.

Miss Renor put a slender, purple-tipped hand slowly

into his. 'How—wonderful!' she murmured, fluttering long lashes Eden couldn't believe were real!

'My pleasure,' Dane said softly, raising the hand clasped in his to his lips.

Eden watched bitterly. He might have had foreign blood in his veins, the way he carried that off! There were two sides to Dane Sutherland. This urbane, sophisticated one wasn't one she was unfamiliar with but it was so long since she had seen it that she had nearly forgotten. Watching the dark head bent over the long, white fingers, she realised he was devastating enough to capture any woman's imagination, even one as worldly as Miss Renor.

'Would you like to dance with me, so I can tell you about my cousin?' smiled Miss Renor, with a confidence that must surely match his own. 'I have a few minutes before I'm on again.'

'Enchanted!' Eden heard Dane murmur as she ground her teeth.

Unable to keep her eyes off them as they circled the floor, she heard her mother saying as she sank into the chair Dane had vacated. 'She begged to be introduced, Eden, I'm sure you don't mind?'

'No, why should I?' What did her mother expect her to say? All she could do was grin and bear it. She could hardly make a scene with half the tent looking on, with obvious interest! She glanced at her mother quickly. 'Rather a big name to have here, though?'

'Oh, I don't know,' Irene replied absently. 'Someone on the committee happened to meet her and she agreed to come. It was as simple as that.'

Nothing would be that simple with Clare Renor! Thrusting something niggling at the back of her mind aside, Eden's unhappy glance gravitated towards her again. Dane was holding her so tightly there couldn't be a hair's breadth between them. They weren't dancing conventionally, either. Both Dane's arms were around the girl while hers were crossed behind his neck. They weren't moving much, they were simply in a clinch.

Eden felt something choke in her throat and turned away, feeling sickened.

'I—saw in the paper that her divorce came through a few weeks ago.'

'Yes,' Irene was following the couple's performance, too, but with more satisfaction than Eden. 'It caused quite a stir, I believe.'

'In what way?'

'Don't you remember?' Irene sounded mildly surprised. 'She has two children but didn't apply for custody. They're living with their father.'

Eden frowned, realising this was what she had been trying to remember. 'Surely that's unusual?'

'Yes, well,' Irene paused, 'that's what the media thought too. They made quite a thing of her saying she wasn't fond of children, but not everyone is. I think she ought to have been admired, not condemned for not being afraid to be honest.'

'Mother!' Eden exclaimed, as something more important came back to her. 'What did you mean about Dane being Burford Oils?'

Irene smiled faintly. 'Haven't you seen your father yet? He's discovered Dane's the chairman and major shareholder and seems to have diversified in other directions as well.'

'I thought he just worked for them?' Eden whispered.

'Not any longer, it seems.'

While Eden was recovering from the shock of this, Irene glanced at her contemplatively. 'He's still not as wealthy as Trevor's going to be, when his father dies. And I know Ben Lawson's health's not very good.'

Eden's soft lips compressed. Didn't Irene understand anything! Hadn't she learned, after all this time, that her daughter considered other things far more important than money. She rubbed her fingers distractedly over her burning forehead. What had gone wrong between Dane and herself since the weekend? She couldn't have imagined his passion and warmth at the cottage, yet everything he had done and said since seemed to deny it. Blinking back tears, she sought out his tall figure and found him escorting Clare back to the stage before returning to join them.

'Such a nice girl!' Irene began cooing, even before he sat down. 'She's talked to me a lot during these past few days—she's been coming here for rehearsals, you know, and, despite her success, life seems to have dealt her some very hard blows.'

'Artists like Clare can be extremely vulnerable,' Dane agreed heavily.

He was talking above their heads. Eden didn't think his eyes had left the stage. 'Care to dance?' he asked Eden carelessly, barely glancing at her.

'Why not?' she agreed. She had been about to refuse but it might be her last chance to be in Dane's arms.

Her mother said, as she stood up, 'I'll see you later, dear. I must go and find your father. The naughty man is probably still entrenched in his study!'

Dane had held Clare Renor as close as seemed possible but Eden didn't expect, or even want the same kind of treatment herself. Not in such a public place, anyway! She need not have worried. He held her so impersonally, she might have been just anybody, which unwisely provoked her to remark, with sarcastically curling lips, 'Miss Renor performs remarkably well on the floor.'

'Umm. She dances as well as she sings,' Dane praised warmly, edging Eden nearer to where Miss Renor was crooning meltingly, *When Will I See You Again?*

'How—nice!' Eden muttered.

Dane grinned tauntingly. 'She may even be talented in other directions?'

'Do you intend finding out?'

'Would you care?' he countered flatly.

Did he expect her to sink her pride altogether, by confessing how much! 'You are quite free to do as you please,' she replied stiffly.

He murmured softly. 'When a woman's as beautiful as Clare Renor, she is very difficult to resist.'

'Why try?'

He gazed into her stricken eyes, reading something in them to keep his diverted from the stage. His voice curiously urgent, he exclaimed, 'At the weekend, Eden . . .'

'Don't give it another thought,' she broke in with a forced laugh, as she thought she understood what he was trying to say. She pretended an indifference which she hoped seemed completely genuine. 'Old ties aren't necessarily good ones, Dane, as many discover when they attempt to take up where they left off.'

'You're being very tolerant,' he snapped, 'considering everything.'

Glancing at him quickly, Eden was surprised by the sudden paleness of his face. What else could she be? she asked herself bleakly. Surely the least she could do was to try and make things easy for him? If she'd had any rights, what use would they have been when he didn't love her? She could sense some kind of disturbance in him, which must be the attraction he felt for Miss Renor? Lucky Miss Renor! Eden thought bitterly.

She heard Dane's breath rasp but when he spoke again he was breathing evenly. 'I would still feel a bit of a heel, leaving you.'

His conscience was pricking him. Eden winced, wondering if she was courageous enough to dismiss it for him? 'You don't have to worry about me,' she assured him lightly. 'You heard my mother saying how devoted I am to my shop,' she had to pause before she could manage more lies, 'and my life in London. And I could be tempted to have another go at matrimony, myself. Trevor . . .'

Dane demanded incredulously. 'After what Lawson did, to both of us, you'd forgive him?'

'Well . . .' Eden stammered with bent head, 'I've been thinking. Has he really done anything but try to prove his devotion? Perhaps not always as he should have done, I admit, but maybe it's time I began making allowances?'

'I can't believe I'm hearing properly,' Dane exploded grimly.

'Haven't you ever deceived anyone, Dane?' she retorted.

He hesitated, eyes darkening. 'If I have, I've never gone in for the kind of deception Lawson practises.'

Not even when you didn't mention owning Burford Oils? she almost said but didn't. It must have happened since their marriage broke up and he would be quite justified in pointing out that it was none of her business. 'Some of us might be worse than others,' she allowed with a giggle.

Dane didn't appear to realise she wasn't amused so much as hysterical. 'Yes,' he rejoined roughly, 'but when you defend someone, as you do Lawson, he has to mean a lot. Perhaps it is time we both got ourselves sorted out?'

Numbly she nodded. It was perhaps better that Dane believed she loved Trevor, rather than him? If she confessed how much she loved him, she shuddered to think of his probable embarrassment. Her feet stumbled as the dance finished and his hand nearly broke her arm in two as he guided her back to their table.

'I think I'll go and see if my father's been found yet,' she said hastily, searching frantically for an excuse to escape before Clare returned. Somehow she felt unable to face seeing them together again.

Clare was in the middle of another number, even more haunting than the last, but Dane confused Eden by not sparing the singer a second glance.

'I'll take you to him,' he snapped, 'I don't want you wandering about in the dark.'

'It's only a short distance to the house,' she objected, but he took no notice. A few minutes later, she found herself outside with him but instead of walking towards the house, he bewildered her by almost thrusting her into the shade of some nearby trees. Here, to her continuing astonishment, he turned in the darkness and pulled her forcibly into his arms, silencing her further inarticulate protests with the bruising pressure of his marauding mouth.

CHAPTER TEN

His kisses were ruthless and contemptuous. Eden tried to fight him but she could do nothing against his fury and strength. Gone was all the tenderness and gentle passion he had shown her at the weekend. He assaulted her vulnerable lips violently, taking what he wanted with no regard for the right or wrong of it, or concern for her bruised emotions. It didn't help either, when she found she had stopped struggling and was returning his plundering kisses hungrily, her mouth parting to the insistence of his, her arms going tightly around his neck.

Their tongues were duelling as he began swiftly undoing the buttons on the front of her dress and his hands travelled intimately over her soft breasts and along the curves of her slender waist and hips. She felt her whole body dissolving wildly at his touch, so that it came as a terrible shock to find herself suddenly thrust abruptly away from him.

'Dane?' she gasped, failing to appreciate her freedom as she gazed blindly into his cruel face. 'Why . . .?'

'Maybe to finally get you out of my system,' he rasped. 'I think a little violence is as good a way as any.'

Eden stared at him for another horrified moment before fleeing from him in a kind of panic. She didn't stop until she was beside a 'phone. Picking it up, she managed to call a taxi, then continued on her way to her father's study, to tell him she was going.

He wasn't there so she left a note and stayed hidden until she guessed the taxi should have arrived. It was waiting and after saying goodbye to Briggs, who was still on duty, she climbed into it and gave the driver her address. She didn't notice the tall man standing in the shadows, watching her departure, a frozen expression on his face.

All night Eden kept telling herself Dane would come home. Through the long hours until dawn, she prayed he would but she didn't have to open his bedroom door the next morning to know his bed hadn't been slept in. For a long time she stood in her short cotton nightgown and bare feet, her eyes closed, trying to keep back the tears which welled behind her closed lids. Sobs rose to her throat and she restrained them too, until her whole body seemed to ache from the effort.

So she had finally lost him. Though she had been aware it might happen, she had never been completely prepared for it. The awful, shattering realisation that Dane had left her forever took a while to penetrate but when it did she covered her face with both hands to smother a cry like that of a wounded animal. She had never guessed it could hurt so excruciatingly to see all her hopes of a happily fulfilled future reduced to nothing, like so much dust! Dane must have stayed with Clare Renor, last night, for where else had he to go? He couldn't have gone to a hotel with nothing but what he stood up in and the party would have been over hours ago.

A shower helped her to get hold of herself and, after dressing, she woke Jonathan. 'You have to come to the shop with me, this morning, darling,' she said to the small, pyjama-clad figure curled under the sheets, her taut voice reflecting her state of mind.

'Why, Mum?' Jonathan didn't usually argue but he often demanded to be given a reason when asked to do something. 'Why can't I stay with Dad?'

'Because he isn't here,' she replied, 'and might not be for a few days. Now come on,' she added quickly, before he could ask any more questions, 'there's your clothes. I've put out the T-shirt you like with the tigers on it.'

Over breakfast he was still inclined to be stubborn. 'If Dad's not here, Mum, couldn't I stay with Mrs Willis or Peter and his mum?'

'Not today, darling.'

'Oh, all right,' he heaved an enormous sigh and got on with his cornflakes.

Eden looked at his bent head, so like Dane's, in despair. Was she being a coward? keeping from him that Dane wasn't coming back, that he wouldn't be seeing him again, at least, not here. She would have to tell him sometime but she didn't want him to learn the hard way, which, undoubtedly, was the way it would be if she allowed him to stay at the flat and Dane arrived to pack his things.

'I miss Dad, Mum.'

Didn't they both! 'Yes,' she replied huskily, knowing that Jonathan had pictured the future much as she had seen it—the three of them together, a baby brother or sister, eventually. Jonathan might be too young to realise such dreams seldom come true but she was old enough to have known better.

'Will he be here when we get back from the shop, Mum?'

'Perhaps. He has business which may keep him away a while.' Beautiful business, she thought hollowly, with a voice like an angel, who probably hadn't objected in the least to him kissing his wife goodbye! Bitterly Eden licked her tongue over still swollen lips. Well, hadn't she sensed all along that it would only be a matter of time before he left, and if it hadn't been Clare Renor it would have been some other woman. The important issue now, she reminded herself, was Jonathan. How would he feel about living, first with one parent then the other? Dane could offer him so much more than she could but, if he married again, would his next wife like a ready-made son?

'You'd better hurry, darling,' she warned him automatically, 'or I'll be late.'

'Yes, Mum.'

Her heart bled for him. He was such a pleasant child, though she said it herself. If only she could protect him from the harsher aspects of life. Surely he was too

young to have to face them yet? The rough patches
might be what boys needed to toughen them up but did
Jonathan deserve what she and Dane were doing to
him?

Her thoughts churned as they walked to the shop.
Maybe next year she could afford a small car and take
him out? Or she could sell up and return to living with
her parents? Jonathan would enjoy the extra freedom,
the extra time she'd be able to give him and her parents
would be overjoyed to have them. No, she shook her
head so emphatically that another pedestrian glanced at
her curiously. That would be too much like admitting
defeat. Dane and she would have to discuss Jonathan's
future properly. She sighed at the thought of lost
opportunities. Dane would probably collect his clothes
from the flat while she was out, so she wouldn't see him
and any communication they had, in future, might be
through his solicitor. She glanced at the sky unhappily
as a large raindrop fell on her face. Dark clouds were
forming which didn't seem like a good omen. She
supposed, in time, her battered emotions would finally
become numb, until she felt nothing, but right now she
seemed to be hurting more than she could bear.

Jonathan played upstairs while she opened the shop
but he soon tired of his games and came down to
plague her with more questions. Usually she didn't
mind for she liked his enquiring mind, but she hated
him asking questions she couldn't answer—or had no
answer she could give without hurting him.

'Are we going to live with Dad, Mum? Is he away
looking for a house for us?'

'I'm not sure what he's doing,' she replied unevenly,
thinking privately that that would be the last thing!

'I liked the cottage,' Jonathan's eager voice ran on.
'It's just a nice size. If I had some brothers and sisters it
might not be but I don't think I'd like to live in a huge
mansion. Peter says they're usually haunted.'

Eden was saved from answering, this time, by Leo's
arrival. 'Florence sent me around,' he confessed, after

Jonathan, believing his mother would be occupied for a while, disappeared upstairs again. 'The two of us,' Leo resumed gruffly, 'have been having a good talk and we wondered if it would be possible to approach you without appearing to be pushing our noses into your business, so to speak?'

'Try me?' she couldn't help smiling at such nervousness from a man who was usually outspokenly blunt.

'It's just that,' again he hesitated awkwardly, 'well, as your husband's back. Oh, I know,' he said hastily, as she opened her mouth, 'you're divorced, but we've seen how you look at each other and we wondered, if you did get together again and move on, if you'd consider letting us have the shop?'

Eden looked at him and paled, her voice shook visibly. 'I'm ashamed of the way I feel, Leo. I seem to have lost all my pride. You could have the shop tomorrow if Dane would have me back, but he doesn't want me . . .'

'You still love him?' Leo was his blunt self again.

'Yes.' Please don't let me break down and weep, she silently prayed. 'But he doesn't love me. And I'm beginning to believe there's nothing as dead as a dead love unless, perhaps, one that never happened in the first place . . .'

Leo seemed to follow her muddled thinking precisely and his kindly face creased in concern. 'I'm sorry, child . . .'

'Don't be,' she begged, her eyes unconsciously bleak. 'It's been mostly my fault, I can't really blame Dane. However,' she made an effort to stop trembling, 'if I do think of parting with the shop, for any reason, I'll give you first chance.'

Leo's unspoken sympathy almost proved her undoing but it was comforting to know she had good friends. If she could find another means of earning a living where she could have more time to spend with Jonathan, she would let Leo and his wife have the business and be glad to, but, at the moment, what with unemployment being so high and everything, barring a miracle, she couldn't see it happening.

Dane didn't come to collect his things and by the weekend Eden was so frantic that she accepted the usual Sunday luncheon invitation from her mother. She had to get over Dane, she knew she couldn't go around forever with tears springing to her eyes whenever she thought of him. Jonathan wasn't looking over happy, either, and she needed something to strengthen her. Maybe a bracing quarrel with her mother would do the trick? She refused to admit she was really going because of Dane—in the desperate hope that she might learn what had happened to him?

She was surprised to find Trevor wasn't there when she arrived. He had given her a ring on Friday, asking her out and she'd heard nothing since she had refused, but she hadn't expected her mother to give up as easily. Eden felt warmer towards her than she'd done for a long time, that she seemed at last to be considering her feelings.

To her further surprise, she discovered there were only two other guests besides herself and Jonathan and as these were old friends of the family, she didn't find them a strain. It wasn't until after they had eaten and her father was escorting them around the grounds with Jonathan in tow, that she was able to have a private word with her mother.

'Did you make all the money your charity needed on Wednesday?' she asked casually. 'There were certainly plenty here.'

'Charities never have all they need,' Irene retorted, frowning on a bowl of roses and starting to rearrange them. 'I'm sorry Dane couldn't manage today. He appeared to enjoy himself the other evening.'

'I—I told you, he's away.' Irene had asked them both to lunch.

'So you did! My memory's getting bad. How long did you say?'

'I didn't.'

Irene turned, her voice cool. 'Very well, Eden, if you don't wish me to know anything, I'm used to having a daughter who never confides in me.'

Had she ever encouraged it? Eden stared at her incredulously. All Eden's attempts to talk to her as a child, had met with the same response. 'Some other time, darling!' And, as she'd got older, Irene had been too fond of telling her what she must do. She had only been willing to consider Eden's problems one way, and that had been from her own point of view.

'All right,' she gave in wearily. 'You'd have to know sometime. Dane has gone—he may not be coming back.'

'But, I thought . . .' Irene threw out her hands in apparent dismay, 'Well, he brought you to the party and you seemed happy enough.'

Where were the usual I told you so's? Eden's eyes narrowed on her mother suspiciously but she dismissed her doubts as imagination. For once, Irene was probably trying to be understanding?

'I think,' she said carefully, 'he was attracted to Clare Renor.'

'Who? Ah, yes, I remember,' Irene frowned. 'That is, I did notice he seemed quite taken with her, but then so were a lot of the other men. You know what men are like? He's probably forgotten about her by now, although . . .'

'Yes?' Eden's heart gave a sickening lurch as her mother hesitated.

'Nothing . . .' murmured Irene.

'Mother!'

'Oh, very well!' Irene exclaimed impatiently, 'I didn't intend mentioning it but if you insist! I did hear he had moved in with her. Of course,' she hastened, as Eden went white, 'it could only be a rumour. You can't believe half the things people say.'

'Nothing's impossible.' Eden lifted her chin with pretended indifference. 'We've been divorced a long time, remember. Dane was only staying with me in order to get to know Jonathan.'

'Yes, well,' Irene smiled mysteriously, 'it's no secret that Miss Renor dislikes children.'

Jonathan burst in then, running up to Eden and tugging at her hand. 'Come and see the new duck Grandpa has on his pond, Mum! It has such funny coloured feathers.'

No more was said about Dane or Clare Renor and because Trevor wasn't mentioned, either, Eden stayed with her parents until it was Jonathan's bedtime. This left her fewer hours to brood but, somehow, the shock she had sustained on having it confirmed that Dane was living with Clare Renor, stayed with her. She stopped feeling anything and was functioning nicely on a mind pleasantly anaesthetised by numbed acceptance.

The following afternoon, she decided to close the shop for half a day. Usually she did this on Saturdays, to ensure she had a long weekend to spend with Jonathan but suddenly, during Monday lunchtime, she knew she couldn't go on without a break. Calling Jonathan down from upstairs, she told him what she intended doing and tried not to notice how pleased he was.

'We can go out somewhere, if you like?' she suggested as they reached the flat. She had meant to go through some accounts but it was such a lovely day.

'I'll read the new book Dad bought me, until you're ready,' he said eagerly.

Eden's breath drew in sharply as he spoke of Dane. Would she ever escape him! All the lovely numbness that had taken over disappeared, leaving only pain. Stumbling to the spare bedroom, she gazed around it tearfully. He wasn't there, he never would be again. How many times would she have to do this before she was convinced?

With an impatient sigh, she brushed the tears from her eyes and turned away. In the bathroom she quickly rinsed her face and hands and changed into her jeans.

She was crossing the hall to go to the kitchen when the doorbell rang.

Frowning, she halted in her tracks. It couldn't be Jennifer as she and Peter were on holiday this week. Nor Mrs Willis, who was out for the afternoon. What about Dane? a small voice suggested, which she tersely ignored. It could be half a dozen people, for heaven's sake! She could guess all afternoon, and wasn't it foolish being scared of answering the door for fear it was the one person she longed to see?

All the same, her heart was beating far too fast when she did, and she was more shocked by whom she found standing on her doorstep than she might have been, had it been Dane.

'Brown!' she gasped, feeling everything beginning to spin.

He caught her as she swayed. 'Miss Eden, ma'am!' his voice was as hoarse as hers. 'Are you all right?'

The ceiling stopped threatening to come down on top of her. 'I am now,' she smiled faintly. 'Sorry for being so silly.' She tried for a steadier breath. 'It was such a surprise . . .' And that's no exaggeration! she thought despairingly. What was Brown doing here? What was she supposed to say to him?

He looked embarrassed behind the concern he displayed. 'I didn't expect to see you, either,' he muttered, as if he guessed what she was thinking. Lowering her gently to the chair she kept in the hall, he went to close the door. 'Not that I'm not pleased to see you, Mrs Sutherland. H-how are you?'

Another time Eden might have smiled at the unperturbable Brown stammering. 'Very well,' she whispered. 'And you?'

'Me?' Brown appeared bemused that anyone should trouble to ask. 'I've never felt better.'

She gazed at him, her eyes huge. 'What are you doing in London?'

'Well, I'm usually with the boss, Miss Eden,' he said awkwardly. 'I came down with him from the Shetlands.'

'You did?' she frowned. 'Do you have relations in London, Brown?'

A great grin split his face, as if he considered this a joke too. 'Not that I know of, ma'am. I think they've all disowned me.'

'Where have you been staying, then?' she asked uncertainly.

'Why, at the flat, Miss Eden, the boss's flat, that is. Oh, hell!' grinding his teeth, he clapped a huge hand over his mouth as he mumbled, 'Sorry about the language, ma'am, but I wasn't supposed to tell.'

'About—what?'

'The flat, ma'am! Last night, when Dane told me to collect his things, he said I wasn't to say a word about the flat. He did say it wouldn't be you who'd be here but, all the same, I shouldn't go round blabbing my great mouth off!'

Eden shivered in stunned surprise. So Dane had a flat. Where was it—how long had he had it? 'I suppose you know about us, Brown?' she murmured, her throat suddenly dry, 'Our divorce . . .?'

'Yeah.' He shuffled from one foot to the other. 'Talked to me on Wednesday night, when he got in. Talked a lot that night, he did.'

Eden flushed painfully. 'I didn't mean to deceive anyone—at least . . .'

'Think nothing of it, Miss Eden,' Brown said quietly, 'I always see more than I'm supposed to, if you know what I mean . . .?'

'Isn't there a new woman in Dane's life yet?' Eden couldn't help asking, after a brief silence.

'Not that I know of,' Brown replied soberly. 'He's too busy, for one thing. At the office all hours, he is. If I didn't put my foot down occasionally, he'd never sleep.'

Eden stared at him blindly. So Dane hadn't deserted her for another woman. She hadn't even the comfort of knowing that! He had simply walked out. In other words, he had tired of her; decided they meant nothing to each other, anymore, and that a quick, clean break was the best way. He was ruthless enough to be able to do it and recalling how he had been, the last few days he had stayed here, she couldn't pretend to be really surprised.

Shakily, she stumbled to her feet. 'I'd better go and pack his things, Brown. It won't take long.'

'That's all right, ma'am,' Brown said absently, clearly bewildered by something and, even more so, when Jonathan suddenly charged from the lounge.

Eden had forgotten about him. As she stared at him, a kind of helpless dismay in her face, he looked from Brown to her and his face fell. 'I thought Dad had come home, Mum,' he muttered.

She had never doubted that if Dane had a kind of driver cum bodyguard, Brown had been chosen for his intelligence as much as anything else. One glance at him revealed he realised who Jonathan was. Haltingly she introduced him as Dane's son, knowing it would be useless to deny it. As Jonathan held out his small hand politely, she also tried to explain to him why Brown was here.

'Your father wants some of his things,' she said quickly, 'and isn't able to come himself. If you take Mr Brown into the lounge, I'll go and get them.'

Jonathan hesitated then obeyed. She could hear his eager voice and Brown's rumbling one all the time she hugged each one of Dane's shirts to her before packing it, as though she was saying goodbye to him forever. She returned to the lounge, clutching the bag, unwittingly betraying she had no wish to part with it.

'You've a fine young man, there,' Brown said gruffly, when eventually she handed the bag over and he made for the door.

She followed him out while Jonathan stayed. 'Wouldn't you like a drink, or some tea?'

'No.' He paused awkwardly, 'I think I should get straight back.'

'I understand.' She raised eyes filled with sudden tears. 'How is he, Brown?'

'I'm not sure,' he muttered, watching her distressed face closely. 'Oh,' he added casually, 'by the way, if you ever want me, I've scribbled down the address.'

She went to the bedroom after he left, still clutching the scrap of paper he had thrust in her hands. The past ten minutes had shaken her more than she cared to admit. She felt on the verge of collapse. Why hadn't Dane mentioned having his own apartment, instead of letting her believe he slept at the office or a hotel when he was in London. Why all the secrecy? Questions without answers began plaguing her as she sank on to her bed and buried her face in her hands. If he had gone to his own flat, after the party, had he taken Miss Renor with him? Brown gave the impression he hadn't but, if he had done, would Brown have said?

Yet, Eden pondered bleakly, if Dane hadn't taken Clare anywhere after the party, then it must be as she'd thought before, that he had merely been using her to enable him to make a break from Eden. He must have assumed that if Eden believed he was with another woman, she wouldn't come after him or make a fuss. All this implied that he no longer wanted her—and yet . . .

Eden's smooth forehead creased as she gazed at the opposite wall and screwed up the paper in her hands. Something about all this didn't seem to ring true. Somewhere, along the line, she was suddenly convinced, she had been cleverly misled into acting as she might not otherwise have done if, on the night of the party she had been in possession of a few relevant facts.

After sitting a few minutes longer, deep in thought, Eden jumped up and rushed to the hall. Jonathan was apparently engrossed in a TV game. She told him quietly that she had a call to make and closed the lounge door. It was imperative that she spoke to her mother. With a sinking feeling in her stomach, she lifted the 'phone.

She caught Irene at home. 'Eden!' she exclaimed. 'How nice to hear from you.'

Eden wasn't bothering with such niceties. She only

wished she'd had someone to take care of Jonathan so she could have gone and talked to Irene, face to face. 'Mother,' she said abruptly, 'I'd like to speak to you about Clare Renor. Did you invite her to the party, last week, deliberately, with Dane in mind?'

There was a cold silence then Irene said tightly, 'I had you in mind, not him, but I really don't know what you're talking about?'

'I think you do!' Eden's voice was equally chilly.

'Well, what if I did?' Irene suddenly seemed to lose patience. 'Someone had to do something, and no one else seemed willing. And doesn't the fact that Dane fell for Clare like a ton of bricks, prove I was right?'

'It proves you were very foolish, Mother. Maybe worse than that, if I could understand everything . . .'

'My God! Eden,' Irene broke in furiously, 'you must be the most ungrateful girl alive. Don't you see? I did it for your own good!' Her voice shook with a note of self-righteousness. 'I've always been brighter than you. You're far too sentimental to be able to think clearly.'

'Too much heart and no brain, you mean?'

Ignoring this, her mother said brittly. 'You still don't understand, do you, and it's not very difficult. Clare Renor hates children. Well, perhaps that's putting it a bit strongly, but she doesn't pretend they have any place in her life. So if Dane and she have got together, don't you see what that means? He won't be bothering to try and claim Jonathan for she wouldn't have him at any price!'

I don't believe it! Eden thought dazedly. Aloud, she exclaimed, 'You thought all this up?'

'I told you, someone had to,' Irene mistook the incredulity in Eden's voice for admiration, 'I met her by chance and the idea came to me . . .'

'How much did it cost you?' Eden asked hollowly.

'It would have been worth it at twice the price!' Irene replied revealingly. 'Now you can get together with Trevor, which might almost repay me.'

Eden replaced the 'phone quickly, taking no notice as

a minute later it rang again. Collecting Jonathan, she hustled him from the flat, hearing herself planning where they would go as they left, feeling like two separate people. When they returned she would go and find Dane and try and explain what her mother had been up to. After that it would be up to him.

When they got back and Jonathan was in bed, she left Mrs Willis looking after him and set out again, this time to try and find Dane's flat. Unfortunately, while she sat on her bed, she had unconsciously torn the piece of paper Brown had given her and though Dane's address was still intact, the number on it wasn't.

The area was near the West End but there was no huge high-rise block with a commissionaire who might have helped her. It was a quiet cul-de-sac with tall houses converted into flats. Dane's flat could be anywhere and she couldn't possibly knock on every door.

She hung around until eight o'clock and was just about to leave when a car passed her and drew up a few yards away. Realising it was Dane, she smothered a strangled cry and stumbled towards him. The September evenings were drawing in and he didn't immediately notice her approaching, but when he did his face went pale.

'Eden!'

She halted beside him, her own colour receding, unable to look at him. Suddenly she wondered why she was here and had to force herself to say, 'I had to see you, Dane.'

He didn't reply and his silence raised her head. She found him gazing at her, a dazed expression in his eyes. 'I was coming to see you, Eden,' he muttered hoarsely. 'I've just left Brown.'

What had Brown to do with it? 'He gave me your address,' she admitted, 'but I didn't ask for it. I've spoken to my mother since then, though, and I—well, I wanted to speak to you about something.'

His eyes never left her face but from being struck motionless, he was suddenly galvanised into action.

Tightly gripping her arm, before she could protest, he rushed her into a nearby house, up a wide flight of carpeted stairs to the upper apartment. Once they entered it, he slammed the door behind them.

As a bewildered Eden watched it rock on its hinges, he turned to her fiercely. 'Brown thought you looked ill.'

'Brown d-did?' she stammered.

A muscle jerked in the side of Dane's mouth. 'He's been at the office for the past hour, trying to convince me of a few things.'

'Such—as?'

Dane's eyes burned into hers. They were black and seemed on fire. She had never seen him like this before and was shocked at the change in him after only a few days. He replied flatly, like a man without hope. 'I told him it was nonsense, but he believes you love me.'

Eden shrank with shame. Had it been that obvious? 'What makes him think that?'

'Jonathan.'

'J-Jonathan?'

'He heard you talking to Leo at the shop.' Suddenly Dane tightened his grip on her savagely, his face contorted. 'Eden,' he rasped harshly, 'can we, for once, have the truth? You've put me through enough hell since I've known you, for me to feel justified in asking. Did Jonathan get it wrong, or did you really tell Leo you loved me?'

Eden's arms would be bruised but she wasn't conscious of physical pain. 'What good would loving you do me?' she evaded, 'when you don't love me.'

'Are you crazy!' Dane exclaimed thickly. 'I've always loved you. Maybe, at the beginning,' he allowed grimly, 'I didn't recognise the hold you had on me as such, but I do now.'

She stared at him incredulously. His voice was laced with pain. She searched his face, seeing what she'd never thought to see. 'Did you never guess how I felt about you?'

'No,' he shook his head. 'I didn't, and I want to hear you say it.'

'I love you,' she whispered, tears running down her cheeks as it all got too much for her. 'Didn't you know? Oh, darling!' she sobbed, despairingly.

'Don't!' he pulled her closer, recognising the same urgency in her as he felt in himself. They were both so eager to make love that nothing else mattered. There was a mutually revealing moment, as their eyes locked and then he was holding her tightly against the trembling length of his body, his mouth closing over hers.

He kissed her gently at first but soon the tempo of his kisses changed and he was lifting her, carrying her to his bedroom. 'We have a lot to talk about,' he murmured barely intelligibly into her ear, 'but it will have to wait.'

He dropped her on to the huge bed. 'Take your clothes off,' he said huskily, beginning to do the same, 'I want to see you.'

Obediently, Eden pulled off her shirt and jeans but when it came to her underthings she still felt shy with him. With tender understanding, he sank down beside her and unhooked her bra himself and removed her brief satin panties.

'You're beautiful,' he said thickly. 'I always want you until I can't think of anything else. How do you feel about marrying me again?'

Such a volume of emotion washed over Eden she could barely speak. These were words she had never expected to hear. 'I thought you would never ask,' she murmured huskily.

'I'll tell you about that, too,' he promised, pushing her over the bed so he could stretch out by her side. 'Later.'

His mouth sought hers and she made a little sound of happiness and moved closer against him. She could feel her body on its own volition move up the bed beside him, her arm weaving around his neck. She couldn't remember feeling so peaceful and aroused at the same time.

His eyes devoured her body between kisses so passionate Eden's head was soon swimming. He seemed absorbed with her curves as though he had never known them before. His mouth sought her breast, her long slender legs and rounded hips until she was overwhelmed by desires that threatened to consume her. She wanted him so much that every moment became a lifetime of exquisite agony. Dane seemed as desperate as she was but bent on fanning the flames inside them to an intolerable heat. All her pent up longing for him exploded as she returned his fevered kisses and, as he lowered his head and his tongue found her hardened nipples, she groaned aloud and began trembling violently, willing to do anything he wished.

Then, when at last he took her, she found herself clinging to him wildly as all control vanished under the waves of dizzying rapture which engulfed their frenzied bodies. Within minutes she was whirled off into space, conscious only of being transported further and more intensely than she had ever been before. Lightning-like shock streaked through her and she heard herself cry out Dane's name as her whole being dissolved in a flood of unbearable rapture.

For a long while they clung to each other afterwards, not speaking until the turmoil in their exhausted bodies subsided a little, making speech possible.

Dane raised his head at last, gazing down on her. 'This is how it's going to be for the rest of our lives,' he said thickly.

'You think I've nothing better to do?' she teased weakly.

'Brat!' he slapped her bare bottom playfully then buried his face in her neck and groaned, 'To think I nearly lost you!'

'I thought it was the other way round,' she murmured. 'I thought you were living with Clare Renor and weren't coming back.'

He looked at her incredulously. 'You can't be serious?'

Eden flushed. 'You didn't come home that night and you seemed very taken with her. What else could I think?'

'I pretended to be taken with her,' he corrected slowly, 'because I was trying to discover if you had any real feelings for me. You see, when we first knew each other, I didn't think the strong effect we had on each other was love. Not that I believed then that there was such a thing, anyway. If you had been older, I would have settled for an affair.'

'You must have felt trapped when I seduced you?' she broke in.

'Who seduced who, I wonder?' he said drily, brushing tender fingers over her hot cheek. 'I don't think I was actually complaining,' he teased. 'You were such a tempting morsel I couldn't resist you. I saw, with hindsight, that the conflict that built up between us after we were married was mostly my fault. I was too absorbed in my work not to feel pulled two ways. The Middle East, where I finally made enough to acquire my own companies, needed all my attention and energy. Or so I thought. But this was why, when you demanded a divorce, I agreed.'

As pain flashed over her face, he kissed her remorsefully. 'Don't think you were the only one who suffered, my darling. I soon realised my mistake but by then you had gone back to living with your parents and I seemed to have little to offer by comparison. I decided you'd been too young to know your own mind and were better off without me. But,' his face darkened, 'if I'd known you were pregnant, nothing on earth would have kept me from you.'

'You never married anyone else.'

'How could I,' he muttered grimly, 'when I couldn't get over you? I did go out with other women but only, I'm ashamed to say, for one purpose, and even that was always a disappointment as nothing ever came near to measuring up to what I'd had with you. Yet it wasn't until you appeared on Shetland that I realised exactly what I had thrown away. Learning I had a son was only a small part of it. I followed you to London, knowing I couldn't let you go. I wanted to marry you again but I was wary, for several reasons.'

'Such as?' Eden whispered, almost breathlessly.

His mouth curved faintly. 'Such as discovering I couldn't face it unless you loved me as much as I loved you. Which was why I daren't let you get too close.'

She trembled in his arms. 'I thought you didn't even like me?'

'Oh, I liked you well enough,' he smiled crookedly. 'On Shetland, I couldn't accept that you'd changed from an enchanting but rather irresponsible teenager, intent on having her own way, to a charming, responsible young woman. In London, when I saw everything you'd done, the way you'd become independent of your parents and brought our son up alone, I felt very humble. I wanted to love you to distraction and to make up to you for everything I'd done to you, but I couldn't be sure you really wanted me. I believed, despite what there seemed to be between us, that you might have transferred your affections to Lawson.'

Eden reached up to push her fingers contritely through his dark hair. 'There's never been anyone but you, Dane. I never even began loving Trevor, or gave him any encouragement other than friendship. My mother . . .'

Dane nodded, as she broke off in angry mortification. 'I think I understand, darling. After our weekend at the cottage, when I couldn't make you jealous of Jennifer, Clare Renor seemed too good an opportunity to miss. I suspected your mother of having a hand in it somewhere but I was getting so desperate that I was willing to try anything that might help me to gauge the depth of any feelings you had for me. When you merely appeared to hate me more, I thought the time had come to get out.

'I saw you leave in a taxi and was just about to leave myself, when Clare caught up with me and asked if I'd take her home? Maybe that was what started the rumours you heard, as I felt I could hardly refuse, but she certainly was never here, nor did I enter her apartment. I escorted her to her door and told her I was still in love with my . . .' he suddenly grinned, 'ex-wife.'

'In the course of conversation?' Eden teased but her eyes were misty. 'She mustn't have told my mother.'

Dane smiled grimly. 'She wouldn't wish anyone to know that not every man is putty in her hands, but I wouldn't touch her with a barge pole.'

Eden, actually beginning to feel sorry for the girl who had caused her so much heartache, began telling him haltingly of the telephone conversation she'd had with her mother. 'I don't think I'll ever be able to forgive her,' she finished bitterly, 'she has such an absurd obsession about Trevor.'

Dane said soothingly. 'This time, when we're married, I'm sure she'll soon come round. Anyway, you can safely leave her to me. I think Irene and I understand each other. You never know,' he added with a grin, 'she may even become fond of me and it could prove handy to have someone to leave the children with, when we're going somewhere where we can't take them with us?'

Eden murmured, eyes dazed with pleasure. 'Children, travel, marriage . . .'

'Not necessarily in that order,' he teased.

'Oh, Dane.' Eden moved so she could look up into his face. 'You don't know how jealous I've been.' She flushed a little with shame. 'That dark-eyed nurse in Shetland, Jennifer, Clare. I thought I was going out of my mind. After your accident, when I realised how much you meant to me, I wanted to be your wife again but I was determined, this time, to leave the proposing to you. I was terrified to give you even a hint of how I felt, for fear you should feel obliged to ask me.'

'Oh, my love,' he breathed, his body stirring, 'if only you had! When I think of all the time we've wasted.'

As his hand curved her chin, so he could kiss her, she suddenly remembered something and drew back. 'What did Brown say, exactly?'

Dane smiled, his eyes on her mouth. 'Just that Jonathan had asked him to give me his love—and yours. When Brown looked a trifle uncertain, Jonathan had assured him that he knew you loved me for he'd heard you talking to Mr Farndale in the shop, and you'd been crying. Brown had somehow got this impression, as well, at the flat, and when he found me at the office and,' Dane hesitated with a wry quirk, 'informed me in rather colourful terms, just what kind of a fool I'd be if I let you slip through my fingers again, I knew I had to see you, if there was even the slightest hope. To find you in the street, obviously looking for me, seemed too good to be true.'

Eden's blue-grey eyes shone softly. 'I loved you in Cairo, here and in France, but never as I do now.'

'You'd better be sure,' he threatened huskily, 'as I'm never going to let you go again.'

Eden knew they still had things to discuss but as he began kissing her again, she decided it was time she got her priorities right. As Dane had said before, there was nothing that couldn't wait. Later they would return to Jonathan and, during the following days, have to more or less rearrange their lives, but nothing was impossible, not when two people loved each other as Dane and she did. With a contented sigh, that feathered his eager lips, she put her arms around him and began returning his demanding kisses, with an answering ardour which at last seemed to satisfy him.

Hello!

You've come to the end of this story and we truly hope that you enjoyed it.

If you did (or even if you didn't!), have you ever thought that you might like to try writing a romance yourself?

You may not know it, but Mills & Boon are always looking for good new authors and we read every manuscript sent to us. Although we are proud to say that our standards are high and we can't promise every aspiring author success, unless you try you'll never know whether one of those new authors could be you!

Who knows, from being a reader you might become one of our well-loved authors, giving pleasure to thousands of readers around the world. In fact, many of our authors were originally keen Mills & Boon readers who thought, "I can do that" — and they did! So if you've got the love story of the century bubbling away inside your head, don't be shy: write to us for details today, sending a stamped addressed envelope. We'd really like to hear from you!

The Editors

Please write to:

Editorial Dept
Mills & Boon Ltd
15-16 Brook's Mews
London W1A 1DR

The Puppet Master   Pacific Disturbance
PIPPA CLARKE   VANESSA GRANT
The Iron Heart   Once More with Feeling
EDWINA SHORE   NATALIE SPARK

Four brand new titles, from four brand new authors.
All in one attractive gift pack for just £4.40, published
on 9th August.
Fall in love with Mills & Boon's new authors.

The Rose of Romance

ROMANCE

Next month's romances from Mills & Boon

Each month, you can choose from a world of variety in romance with Mills & Boon. These are the new titles to look out for next month.

BITTER ENCORE Helen Bianchin
LION OF DARKNESS Melinda Cross
INNOCENT PAWN Catherine George
GIVE ME THIS NIGHT Vanessa James
PERMISSION TO LOVE Penny Jordan
LEAVING HOME Leigh Michaels
THE DEVIL'S PRICE Carole Mortimer
MAGIC IN VIENNA Betty Neels
ICE INTO FIRE Lilian Peake
FATAL DECEPTION Sally Wentworth
*****A WILL TO LOVE** Edwina Shore
*****WILDERNESS BRIDE** Gwen Westwood

Buy them from your usual paperback stockist, or write to: Mills & Boon Reader Service, P.O. Box 236, Thornton Rd, Croydon, Surrey CR9 3RU, England. Readers in South Africa-write to: Mills & Boon Reader Service of Southern Africa, Private Bag X3010, Randburg, 2125.

*These two titles are available *only* from Mills & Boon Reader Service.

Mills & Boon
the rose of romance

YOUR OPINION IS WORTH
A FREE
MILLS & BOON ROMANCE
TO US

Spare a few moments to answer the questions
overleaf, and we will send you an exciting
Mills & Boon Romance as our thanks.

We want to know what you think.

We are always looking for new and appealing ways to
bring you the very best in romantic fiction, ways that
suit your lifestyle and offer you good value for money.

We are now interested in the idea of "talking books",
or sound recordings of our romantic novels. But
before we go any further, we would like to know what
you think of the idea.

The same moving stories with the same high quality,
but listened to rather than read: please help us to
develop this bright new concept by completing the
simple questionnaire overleaf.

Don't forget to fill in your name and address — so we
know where to send your FREE BOOK.

▶SEE OVER ▶▶▶▶SEE OVER▶▶▶▶ SEE OVER▶

Just answer these simple questions for your FREE BOOK.

1. **How do you feel *in general* about the idea of a Mills & Boon book on cassette?**
   Like a lot ☐   Like moderately ☐   Neutral ☐
   Not much interested ☐   Not at all interested ☐

2. **Would you prefer the book to be read as a book or acted as a play?**
   Read as a book ☐   Acted as a play ☐   Don't mind ☐

3. **For a reading as a book, would you prefer a male or female voice?**
   Male ☐   Female ☐   Don't mind ☐

4. **Would you like there to be some background music?**
   Yes ☐   No ☐   Don't mind ☐

5. **Do you listen to plays on the radio now?**
   Every week ☐   Occasionally ☐   Only now and then ☐   Never ☐

6. **If you had a Mills & Boon cassette, where would you listen to it? (Tick all)**
   In the house
   In the car
   Elsewhere, please say ....

7. **If in the house, would it be**
   Just to listen to by itself ☐   Whilst doing other things ☐

8. **What price range would you feel would be reasonable for a Mills & Boon Romance book cassette?**
   Under £2 ☐   £2-2.49 ☐   £2.50-2.99 ☐   £3 or more ☐

9. **Which age group are you in?**
   Under 35 ☐   35 and over ☐

Please post this off today.

Fill in your name and address, put this page in an envelope (you can fold it if you need to) and post today to:

Mills & Boon Book Cassette Survey
FREEPOST,
P.O. Box 236, Croydon, Surrey CR9 9EL

NO STAMP NEEDED

Name _____

Address _____

_____

_____ Post Code _____

BC1